WINTER VIKING

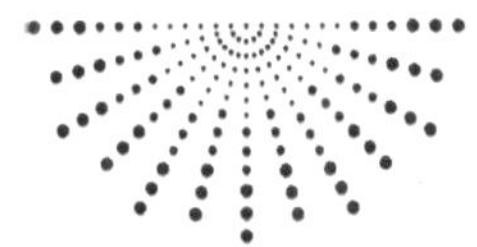

REE THORNTON

DEDICATION

Till min kära Marika som jag älskar och som alltid har trott på mig.

A NOTE ON HISTORICAL ACCURACY

Winter Viking is inspired by the Sámi people whose ancestral lands (Sápmi) include the northern parts of Sweden, Norway, Finland and the Kola Peninsula in Russia. A few years ago, I visited the Ájtte Museum in Jokkmokk and discovered that the rich complex history and culture of the Sámi people is as inspiring as their commitment to the preservation of their traditions in the face of adversity.

For the sake of clarity: there are very few written references to the Sámi peoples during the Viking age and none are from a Sámi perspective. Therefore, some creative licence was taken, with the utmost respect and good intentions, to build the world and story for Ásta and Dànel's journey.

The following facts were used as inspiration:

- The Sámi people's skill as boat builders which is mentioned in the Norse Sagas (Borgarting & Eidsivating 1067-1120), inspired me to write a hero returning to take over his brother's shipping trade.
- Though not renowned warriors like the Vikings, the Sámi were exceptional hunters, using bow and

arrows, spears, and various traps and snares. My
hero's prowess with the bow and arrow pays tribute
to the traditional skills of the Sámi people.

- As a semi-nomadic people, the Sámi moved between
winter and summer lands to graze their reindeer
herds. It is a tradition which continues to this day.
The journey to the summer hut was inspired by this
tradition.
- Like my hero, some Viking boys were fostered out to
forge bonds between two families, however there are
no records of Sámi children being fostered with
Vikings.

I hope you enjoy Ásta and Dànel's story as much as I enjoyed
writing it! And if you have the opportunity, I highly recommend
supporting culturally responsible Sámi tourism to experience
Sámi hospitality and the wonderous beauty of the Sápmi
landscape.

CHAPTER ONE

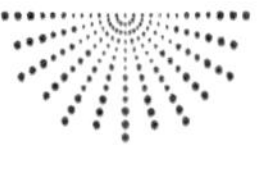

ÁSTA

The rough fibers of the rope cut the tender flesh of Ásta's wrists as the Viking captain yanked her into the sod hut. Her heart pounded in her ears, drowning out all the noise from the village outside. It was time to face what she had done.

"Found this one stowed away after we left Luleavst. Little liar planned to thieve and skip off at the next port. I would have tossed her overboard, but she claimed to know you," said the captain, shoving her forward as if she were a disobedient thrall.

A chorus of disapproving murmurs broke the silence that hung heavy after the captain's accusation.

Ásta fell to her knees, flinching as a stray twig dug into a knee from beneath the soft hides that covered the floor. It would bruise, but it hurt less than her nose, which was almost numb. Why must he live in the wild northlands where it was so cold that it hurt to breathe? Yet again, the gods taunted her by worsening her suffering.

A sudden gust of icy wind slammed the wooden door shut, thrusting the room into sudden darkness.

The aroma of sweet herbs rising from the pot of tea brewing over the waning embers of the fire tickled her nostrils. Was this a steam hut? Ásta inhaled a shaky breath, relishing the sensation of the soothing warm air sliding down her throat. The heat of the fire and steam was a blessed relief to her numb fingers and shivering body. On the long journey north, she had huddled on the longship deck, her thin summer tunic and bedraggled fur proving no match for the blustering icy winds that heralded the beginning of the long dark winter months.

"Shall I take a few of her thieving fingers?" the captain said almost gleefully.

Ásta squinted, her heart racing as she searched for danger in the darkness. She hated being blind almost as much as being backed into a corner—it wasn't safe. As her eyes adjusted to the dim light, she made out eight shadowy figures sitting cross-legged around the fire in the center of the circular room. Who were the hunched old men, and three silver-haired women eyeing her with mistrust?

"Ásta?"

Her shoulders sagged at the familiar rumble of his voice.

"Ásta? Is that you?" Dànel leaned forward, the angular lines of his stubble-covered jaw emerging from the shadows as he threw some wood on the smouldering fire. The sudden flare of firelight illuminated his broad shoulders and powerful arms before he disappeared into the shadows but for his sun-bronzed face and the dark brown eyes that held her captive.

"J-já," she stammered, overcome with relief. She had found him!

Dànel stood and walked toward her. "Get out of my sight," he said to the captain, shooting him a deathly glare as he cut her bindings.

"But—"

"Go," he barked.

Rising to her feet, Ásta rubbed at the chafing on her wrists as she studied the man she had risked everything to find.

Dànel was born of the Sámi, yet he looked every bit the Viking warrior in his loose tunic and breeches compared to the elders clad in reindeer hide garments behind him. Not even the bitter cold stopped him from wearing the front of his tunic unlaced like a Viking, the fabric damp from the sweat that glistened on the hard planes of his broad chest.

Freya help her, he was much larger than she remembered.

Dànel quirked a dark eyebrow at her, waiting for her to speak.

"Well met, Dànel." Ásta wet her parched lips. She'd fought hard to forget the salty musky scent of him and now it was all rushing back. He looked different than he had the night she'd succumbed to her uncontrollable urge to take him to her furs. He'd worn his hair tied back like a Viking then, but now his messy midnight locks fell down past his shoulders.

That wasn't all that was different about him either.

"Why are you here, Ásta?" he said, a muscle jumping in his angular jaw.

Já. He had changed much. A stern caution had replaced the twinkle in his eyes that once matched his easy laughter. Now his straight back and taut shoulders displayed the tension of a man burdened, rather than the playful adventurer who'd straddled two worlds with ease.

"Is what the captain says truth? Did you stow away?" His dark eyes searched hers for answers.

"I did. My pardon for the manner of my arrival," she replied, as the warmth of his gaze began to heat her blood.

Dànel's brow furrowed the longer he looked at her, his full lips pressing into a hard line.

"You're angry. I had hoped that, despite our abrupt farewell, I would find welcome here." Now she realized how wrong she was to have thought that. Dànel knew little of her. They'd only spent that one night together and then she'd rejected him harshly the following morning when the guilt had overwhelmed her. She laced her fingers together over her stomach as a sharp pang hit her in the chest. She ached to trace her fingers across the weathered lines of advancing age on her beloved husband's face. Why did the gods have to take her Njal to Valhalla? She needed him, especially now. She straightened her shoulders and pushed away the thoughts of her beloved before the ache of old grief could settle.

"What of Rúna and Jorvan?" Dànel asked. "Has there been trouble at Luleavst?"

Ásta shook her head. "Nei. All is well at Luleavst. They do not know I am here." She couldn't help but lower her eyes to prevent him seeing her regret. Rúna would be sick with worry at her disappearance. Thank the gods that Jorvan had made his wife promise not to travel while she was with child, for Ásta knew her dearest friend would have followed her as soon as her absence was discovered. After years of hiding, Ásta had known the moment she had locked eyes with the man that had murdered her husband, that the life she had lived in Luleavst was over. Nobody would be safe as long as she remained.

"Why are you here?" Dànel stared at her, his unflinching penetrating gaze that of a man determined to get answers.

Ásta looked at the elderly men and women that had clearly gathered for an important meeting, then back at Dànel. The hair on her arms stood on end. Something wasn't right with him. The death of his brother and returning to his homeland had changed him—he wasn't the man she'd known three moons ago. She glanced over her shoulder at the door. Her whole being insisted she run, get away. She needed to go, *now*.

"Ásta!" Dànel's impatient tone demanded her attention.

Sucking in a shaky breath, she turned and faced him. There was nowhere to go. Her best hope was to plead with Dànel.

"May we speak alone?"

His face remained slack and emotionless. "Why are you here?"

Ásta winced as the truth hit her—any affection he'd felt for her was long gone. She feared what this would mean for her, but she could not blame him. It was she who had taken him to bed and then rejected him, and now she had interrupted an important meeting with her sudden arrival. In truth, she was fortunate that he'd not yet thrown her out in the cold.

Ásta lifted her chin and met his gaze straight on. "I will speak when we are alone."

Dànel shook his head and walked away, his long hair sliding back and forth across his shoulders as he returned to his position by the fire.

She shuffled her feet, itching to step closer to the fire to rid herself of the icy chill that increased the further he moved away.

He looked at her, his dark hooded eyes cold and piercing. "You-will-speak-here." He thrust his finger into the animal skin beneath him as he growled the words at her. "The arrival of an uninvited guest concerns all in the siida."

"I understand," she said, but still hesitated. She knew that she had put him in an awkward position, for she could tell from the tension in the room that he could not allow her arrival to weaken his position or affect his duties to his people. Was she wrong to come to him? Her stomach churned. She'd come here because she thought that she knew how he would react to her secret, but now she was not so sure.

The old woman beside Dànel wrinkled her nose in disapproval, and the men beside her shook their heads and muttered amongst themselves.

Freya help her, she was at the mercy of these people and the mood in the small room had deteriorated from the impending threat of a storm to the loud crashing waves of its arrival.

"Speak, Ásta," Dànel said, his tone sharp.

In a mere heartbeat, Ásta read the warning behind his words

—he could not allow her silence any longer. Gods, how she wished she knew something of the Sami traditions. She could not foresee how these elders would react once they knew her secret, but she doubted that the hospitality she had anticipated would be forthcoming.

"Speak, now!" he demanded.

Ásta straightened her back and steeled herself. She had no choice but to tell him and hope that he would hide her. She cleared the lump in her throat and rested her hands on her stomach.

"I have come because I carry your baby, Dànel."

As the word baby fell from her lips there was a collective gasp and then the silence was absolute but for the crackle and hiss of the fire.

Dànel's eyes widened, and then as realization crept across his face he frowned. His gaze dropped to where she held her stomach, and then snapped back up to her face.

Ásta swallowed nervously, her eyes searching his handsome features for any hint of emotion that would betray his thoughts. Would he be pleased to learn he would be a father?

A muscle in his jaw ticked, telling her everything she needed to know.

Her heart sank. He was furious. What had she been think-ing? He would not take in a woman he'd shared one night with, not even if she was carrying his child.

The deafening quiet in the hut stretched, hanging as heavy as fresh turned earth on a child's grave.

She should never have come here.

Dànel turned and spoke to the elders, clearly translating her words as he locked eyes with each person in the circle.

Ásta lowered her eyes and tamped down the urge to escape as angry chatter she did not understand filled the room. What were the Sami traditions? She'd heard tales of women banished but had never considered that they may be true. Was Dànel seeking their approval to keep her until the baby was born, and then cast her out after the birth? A chill crept up her spine at the thought that she'd created her own entrapment. Her heart ached at the thought of losing another child.

I would rather die.

Curse the gods—coming here was a terrible mistake.

CHAPTER TWO

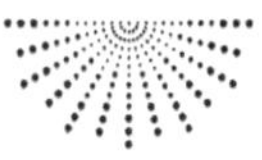

DÁNEL

*L*ong after nightfall, Dànel stepped into his hut and stomped the snow off his boots. It had been a trying day, but he was eager to see the woman that had created such uproar with the elders. His gaze locked on Ásta as he shrugged off his fur coat and hung it on the hook by the door.

She had glanced at him briefly as he entered, but remained seated by the fire, her legs tucked sideways beneath her and her gaze fixed on the dancing flames.

His eyes roamed over the slender curve of her back and graceful tilt of her neck. "Are you well? Have you eaten?"

Gracefully, she rose to her feet and turned to face him.

His pulse leapt at the sight of her pale freckled face, light blue eyes, and auburn hair shimmering in the firelight of his hut. By the gods, he'd forgotten how she made his blood rush. She looked otherworldly, like a gift from the gods delivered to his door. He had desired her the moment he had laid eyes on her in Luleavst, but he wanted her even more now. Deep within him, something stirred and then surged forth. *He needed to keep her.* As fast as the thought arose, Dànel brushed it aside. *Nei!*

That was not him. He did not take or claim women against their will.

"Já. A woman brought me food and lit the fire," she said, straightening her shoulders, her lithe frame taut like a wary warrior. Her guardedness was vastly more than the uncomfortable situation warranted—she was afraid of him.

He frowned and noticed the slight tremble in the hands she held clasped together in front of her body. Why would she fear him? He had given her no cause to think he would harm her.

Sliding off his boots, he placed them near the door to dry before moving toward her.

She remained still, though her eyes followed his forward progress and the tick in her jaw only relaxed when he halted a fair distance away.

"My pardon if I have caused you strife. It was not my intent." She held his gaze, her clenched hands he only sign of her discomfort.

"It matters not," he replied absently, and tore his eyes from hers. A man could lose himself in those orbs the same blue hue as the purest ice. The force with which he wanted her was shocking.

Ásta shook her head and stepped forward cautiously. "It does matter. I do not wish to be a burden for you."

The gentle resignation in her voice made him want to take her in his arms and comfort her. He moved back, needing to put distance between them to calm the heat coursing through his body.

"You are not a problem, Ásta."

"It was unfair to treat you as I did and then come here."

"It was for the best that you ended our liaison." It had hurt his pride at the time, but her severing any hopes he'd had of a connection between them would make living with her over the coming moons and then letting her go when the baby was born, easier. "Do not worry, I shall provide for you and the baby."

Ásta crossed her arms over her chest, providing an enticing view of the tops of her creamy breasts.

He glanced downward, ashamed that he hoped they might fall out of her thin summer dress.

"I am sorry to have made my problems yours. Dànel?"

He raised his eyes and colored as she quirked an eyebrow at him. "You are not a problem." Thankfully she was unaware of the chaos her arrival had caused with his aunts and uncles who believed that their siida was no place for a Viking woman. That Ásta carried his child won her even less favor with the elders, since it had destroyed their plans to marry him to a daughter of the Sidhault siida.

Ásta pressed her lips together in a disapproving line. "Do not lie to me. I saw their faces when they learned I am with child. They disapprove. "

Dànel sighed. She was right. He should have known that she would not accept his attempt to brush her concerns aside and was too clever to believe his clumsy lie.

"All agreed that you will stay until the baby is born," he said reassuringly. They had, after he'd promised to soothe the inevitable tensions with the Sidhault siida, but she didn't need to know that.

Her blue eyes narrowed suspiciously. "How did you convince them?"

He shrugged nonchalantly. It hurt that they denied him the same respect they'd given to Ándde. Despite the years he was absent from the siida while fostered with the Eriksson family, Kvitfjell blood still ran in his veins, and he'd not let them push him from the position he'd inherited from his brother.

"I did not make them see sense. The noaidi insisted that you stay." He unfastened the leather belt that held his sword and dagger, ignoring the prickle of awareness that crept across the back of his neck. He knew that Ásta watched him, her eyes following his every move.

"The noaidi?" Ásta stumbled over the unfamiliar word.

Moving to the bed, he leaned his weapons against the wall where they would be within reach whilst he slept.

"The noaidi is our healer and link to the spirit world. None would dare dismiss Ealjá's council." It was fortunate that Ealjá had learned of Ásta's arrival, for it was his appeal for her to stay that had turned the tide of discontent.

Ásta cocked her head and eyed him cautiously. "What did the noaidi say?"

How much should he tell her?

Ealjá had tossed herbs and water onto the hot rocks around the fire until the room was filled with pungent steam. Everyone's eyes had stung, and their skin was slick with sweat by the time the shaman had began beating his drum and swaying back and forth chanting to his spirit guides.

"He said that the gods had sent the baby as a gift..."

"And?" Ásta prodded.

Dànel's eyes locked on hers. "But there would be a perilous darkness to conquer." He watched Ásta's face pale, until she was as white as fresh snow at dawn. He knew how she felt—the shaman's ominous prophecy had made his skin crawl too.

"W-what else?" she whispered.

"When I find my place, the sun will shine once more."

Ásta swayed slightly, her eyes glassy and her pallid face vacant of emotion.

Damn, he shouldn't have told her. Dànel eyed her suspiciously. She looked like she was going to throw up her meal. Was it the shock or had the harrowing journey exposed to the cold made her sick? She was not accustomed to such extreme conditions. Something was wrong—he could feel it in his gut. Why risk her life, when she could just send word of the baby?

"Why does Rúna not know you are here?" he asked her, now determined to discover why she'd risked the dangerous journey north *and* hid it from her closest friend.

She shifted uncomfortably and stared down at her feet.

The hair on his neck stood on end. She *was* hiding something. Was she running from someone? Mayhap the noaidi's prediction was true and Ásta had fled a darkness that would follow her here.

"Rúna is with child. I could not stay and put her in danger."

A sour taste filled his mouth. "What danger?"

For a few long moments, Ásta avoided his demanding gaze, only relenting when he refused to break the long uncomfortable silence.

"I cannot," she whispered as a log caught fire, the sudden firelight illuminating her face and the distress caused by his questions.

"You must, Ásta." He needed answers. "I cannot shield you from an unknown enemy."

Her eyes widened as he stepped forward, closing the gap between them until he was close enough to see the small freckle in the corner of her lip and feel the heat of her body.

An enticing blush crept across her pale face and neck.

Satisfaction filled him. She was trying to conceal it, but he still affected her. He could tell she was fearful so he spoke to her gently. "Tell me, so I can protect you."

Ásta bit her lip and nodded. "There is a man, a powerful man..."

"Já," he encouraged.

"He wants me. A refusal will mean...death," she whispered, each word barely loud enough for him to hear.

Clenching his teeth, Dànel looked up at the ceiling. He did not want to scare her by revealing his need to punch the man that would threaten a woman, in the face, repeatedly. He released a controlled breath and unclenched his fists. If this coward followed Ásta north, he would gladly show him the error of his ways.

Ásta sucked in a shaky breath, and tears rolled down her cheeks.

His anger melted away at the sight of her misery. "Come," he said, and gently led her to sit beside the fire. Crouching beside her, he rubbed his hand gently across her lower back. "I'll not let anyone hurt you."

Gathering herself, she wiped the tears from her cheeks and then placed a hand on her slightly rounded stomach.

Dànel froze at the visible proof of the life that grew within her. Before him, he was sure she had been alone a long time. And given her reaction afterward, he doubted she would have taken another lover. A child, his child, of that he had no doubt. After Ándde died, he had finally returned to the north only to feel like a stranger in his own family. He did not belong here anymore. His future lay roaming the sea, alone. He'd never expected to father a child, or have a family of his own. He never wanted Ándde's shipping trade, or position in the siida, and now he was responsible for the Kvitfjell lineage too.

"The baby makes me teary."

Dànel shook off his self-pity and lowered himself down beside Ásta. She needed him. By the will of the gods he had returned to the north and she had followed him. He was fated to be here to protect Ásta and provide for her and his child. He reached out to caress the gentle curve that cradled his child safely within.

Ásta's hand snapped around his wrist, her nails piercing his tender flesh.

He froze, his eyes darting to hers, the fury in her glare catching him unaware.

"I'll not let you hurt my baby," she hissed, her words cutting through his tender intent.

He recoiled—shocked she would think him capable of harming his own child. "I would not..." He peeled her embedded nails from his wrist and pushed her hand away.

"Not what?" she spat at him.

Her courage made him smile. She was like a wildcat protecting her cub. "I would never hurt our little one, Ásta. Nor shall I allow anyone to hurt you."

She stilled, studying him intently, before a flicker of hope flashed across her features.

"Promise?"

What in Hel? Dànel kept it from showing on his face, but he seethed on the inside. Who had hurt her? Only a woman who had been abused would ask for such a vow.

Gently cupping her chin in his hand, he looked into her eyes. "No one will ever hurt you. I swear it."

Their eyes remained locked, the moment stretching as he sought to convince her that he could protect her.

Eventually, she pushed her shoulders back and nodded slightly. Even with a pale tearstained face, she looked lovely— her eyes alight with renewed determination.

Unable to resist, he reached out and brushed his thumb across her lips and the curve of her cheek.

Slightly tilting her head, she leaned into the palm of his hand and looked at him through hooded eyes.

"Tell me everything. Who wants to kill you?" he asked, letting his hand fall from her face.

She inhaled a fortifying breath. "He wants me for his wife—"

"Never," Dànel hissed. Nobody would force the mother of his child to wed, not even him. He had never planned to marry, but it would protect her and the baby. Mayhap she would agree to a loveless marriage arrangement for the sake of their child?

"Tell me his name."

Ásta seemed to curl into herself, her chin trembling as she spoke. "King Mattias Helgesen of Jotland."

Dànel jerked backward. "King Mattias?"

She nodded, biting down on her bottom lip so hard he thought she'd draw blood.

A chill crept down his spine. King Mattias was powerful and had a reputation for ruthless brutality. He was not a man you wanted for an enemy. Tales of the king's strange proclivity for blood in the bedchamber were renowned. His gut churned at the thought of Ásta suffering such horrors.

"Did you live at court?" he asked, confused. How had she met the king? And why would he wish to marry a woman of no worth? It made no sense.

"Mattias always coveted me, but he became obsessed when I married his brother." Ásta refused to look at him, her hands fretfully plucking at the hem of her dress.

Dànel jerked back, unable to hide his shock. "Son of Loki! You are no handmaiden." He swallowed hard as the truth hit him like a club to the back of the head.

"Nei." She shook her head. "I wish that I were."

He could barely speak. "You are Queen Ásta of Jottland."

"Já. I am."

Thor's hammer! She was the widow of King Njal Helgesen and a daughter of King Ake Sorensen of Heidabyr. He had bedded a woman of pure royal blood, a queen. Men had hung for less. He was still stumbling over the revelation when Ásta continued with her tale.

"Mattias never cared that I was married to his brother. He often tried to force himself on me." Her eyes glazed over as she recounted the events that had led her here, to him. "Four summers ago Njal and I were travelling to the temple at Uppsala—"

"For the dísablót, the sacrifice?"

"Já. We had had a good harvest and there was much to trade."

"What happened?"

Her eyes filled with tears. "We were ambushed on the road."

Needing to offer her comfort, Dànel reached for her hand, cradling it within his own. "He died in the battle?"

Ásta nodded, the movement unleashing a stream of tears

down her cheeks. "He fought alongside his men. I watched as he took a blade to the chest."

He patted her hand gently. "He now feasts with Óðinn in the halls of Valhalla."

"Já. It is a small comfort. I was wounded and should have died, too, but Rúna pulled me to safety and hid me until we could escape."

"You were fortunate," he said, rubbing her back to encourage her to stay strong long enough to finish her tale.

"Nei." She looked up at him, her eyes heavy with sorrow. "You live."

"What life is this? Hiding from the world, afraid to go outside."

"You survived, Ásta. You are stronger than you think. Now tell me about the king."

"As we hid in the woods, I saw Mattias up on the ridge. For a moment I believed he had come to aid us, but then the two riders beside him rode into the battle and cut down the last of the living. I knew then that Mattias had murdered Njal because he was angry he could not have me." Ásta's chest heaved one last time before she dropped her head into her hands and keening sobs wracked her body.

"It is not your fault," he said in a soothing tone, wrapping an arm around her shoulders and pulling her into his arms. It was unfortunate she had witnessed the murder. The battlefield was no place for a woman, especially not a noble one.

With each anguished shudder of her shoulders, he made plans to avenge her. The man who had murdered her husband and terrified her beyond reason would pay for his treachery.

Eventually, after she had pulled away and wiped the tears from her face, he spoke. "So Rúna took you to Luleavst?"

She nodded. "We knew that if Mattias learned I was still alive I would be in danger. We agreed that it would be best if everyone think I died with Njal."

"So Rúna gave you a new home and a new life."

"Já. She is a good friend. For four years nobody thought to look twice at her handmaiden."

"Until me." From the moment they had met he'd been unable to keep his eyes off of her and he'd made no secret of his interest.

"Já. Until you."

"You had a good life. Why did you leave Luleavst?"

"Mattias was at Valen Eriksson's ascension. That night after we..." A rosy blush warmed her cheeks before she gathered herself and continued. "After you left, I returned to the hall and Mattias saw me. I knew then that he would come for me. Pretending to die to escape him just made him even more desperate to have me."

"Did he tell you that?"

"Nei. He didn't need to. He gave me a choice, wed him or die."

His teeth clenched and his mouth turned sour. Men with too much power were the worst kind.

"Why you? He could have any bride."

"Besides thinking he owns me, he wants me because I know that he killed his brother."

She wasn't making sense. "Brothers killing brothers is not uncommon. Why would it matter?"

"Mattias thinks that if he weds me, he can stop me from telling anyone that he murdered Njal. Njal was beloved by his people—it is likely they will rise up if they discover Mattias murdered him."

"A revolt?"

She nodded solemnly. "Mattias will lose their respect, his power, the kingdom. If I refuse he must kill me to keep his secret hidden."

The hairs on Dànel's arm stood on end and a lump formed in the pit of his stomach. What Ásta knew had the power to topple a kingdom. She was right—King Mattias would stop at nothing to silence her.

"Why would the court believe your word over his?"

"I loved Njal. Nobody would believe I would lie about this."

"Why not return and tell your story?"

Ásta shook her head. "Mattias would have me killed as soon as I crossed into his borders."

Dànel eyed her thoughtfully. Everything she'd said was beginning to fit together. "So when Mattias discovered you were alive, you ran?"

"I had to. I knew that he would never stop hunting me. I returned to Luleavst with Rúna, but I could not stay there. I knew that when Mattias came for me, Rúna would fight. I could not put her in danger."

"So, you came to find me?"

"By then I knew that I carried your child. I hoped that you would help me disappear. Mattias would never think to look for me here."

Dànel nodded at her reasoning, though she was mistaken if she thought that a woman as beautiful as she could disappear anywhere. Even if he ordered his crew not to talk, a few ales would loosen lips enough to reveal the lovely stowaway.

"It was wise to come find me."

"I hope so," she said, and tore her gaze from his.

His admiration for her grew the more he discovered about her. King Mattias was renowned for making others bend to his will, but this tiny brave woman had fought back. She was as brave as any shield-maiden. Somehow, she had outwitted and escaped a man feared by all but the bravest of Viking warriors.

Dànel took her hands in his gently. "Look at me."

Her blue eyes pierced the distance between them.

"You are not alone anymore. We share this child. I will protect you both. Tomorrow we will be wed, so that Mattias will have no claim on you."

Ásta tore her hands from his, the gratitude in her eyes fading. "Nei. I cannot wed you."

A heavy feeling settled in his gut. She was rejecting him, *again?*

"Why not?" He couldn't keep the acerbic tone from his voice.

"I will never wed again. I cannot."

Dànel eyed her warily. He'd expected excuses about how he wasn't a suitable match, not a declaration that she'd never marry again.

"You are still young. Don't you want our child to have a family?"

Ásta met his gaze with a determined look that reminded him of youthful warriors that had not yet learned to cede to the inevitable.

"When Njal died, I vowed to never wed again. I would keep the promise I made to the man I love."

He admired the sentiment, but it was a vow founded in grief, and it could not last. Whether she married him or another, her secret was out and she would be pursued until she had the protection of a husband. A royal woman of childbearing age simply could not remain unwed.

"I would not expect bedding, Ásta. It would be an arrangement merely to keep you safe."

Her blue eyes widened. "You would do that?"

He nodded curtly. "I will do whatever I must to keep you and our child safe."

"You want to marry me?"

Dànel avoided her searching gaze. He couldn't lie to her. A loveless marriage was not what he wanted, not at all.

"If you would be safe."

Ásta cocked her head and studied him curiously, reading the unspoken answer in his words.

"Nei." She shook her head. "I will keep my vow. Marrying me

would not stop Mattias. He would just kill you like he did Njal, and then claim me."

"He will not find you here." He gave up on skirting the truth. He'd deceive her if it would make her his wife and shielded by the law.

"Mattias will *never* stop looking for me."

Dànel bristled. "I will protect you."

"From an army of savage Vikings?" Ásta's tone was light, but her concern valid—Mattias had many warriors under his command. Raising an eyebrow at him, she continued, "I admit I know little of northerners, but I do know they are a peaceful people."

Dànel crossed his arms and frowned. It was true that his people would not fare well against a Viking raid. Mayhap he could call on Rúna and Valen for support? He brushed the thought aside immediately. Nei, even they could not best a king's army.

"There is time yet to discuss the options. You must be tired after your long journey."

Ásta eyed him warily—clearly recognising that his easy acquiesce was out of character. "I'll not change my mind, but I am exhausted."

Dànel stood and offered her his hand. "You can rest on my furs. I will join you soon."

"You will not." She pushed his hand away and rose to her feet, glaring as she stepped forward and closed the gap between them.

"We shall not share furs," she hissed, her eyes blazing with a fury that destroyed any hope he'd had of finding comfort in her arms.

His member stiffened, pushing against his breeches eagerly as he fought back the urge to kiss the frown from her face. Even when angry and defiant, Ásta lit a fire in his loins that tested his resolve. Would tracing his thumb over the hard line of her pink lips soothe the tension there? He leaned in close, until his lips hovered just beyond hers. On this, she would not win—she *would* share his furs.

Ásta stiffened and sucked in a shaky breath. She was still, but her eyes darted around the room searching for an escape.

Gods, she was as jumpy as a stray cat caught stealing from the milk pail. He reached up and brushed a few stray hairs caught on her eyelash aside, continuing even when she flinched as his fingers slid across her skin. She was still afraid of him, but she would soon see that he was no threat.

"Those were your rules, Ásta. Not mine." He tucked the hair behind her ear and pulled away. He would not allow her to treat him as though he was the enemy—he was not Mattias. For now, he would be content to have her share his furs, but he hoped that when she trusted him, she would share her body too.

"In my home we will share all, as is the way of my people."

Ásta pursed her lips in a hard line, her eyes flashing with a ferocity that could have felled a Viking army.

"I have no desire to bed an unwilling woman, Ásta," he said, to reassure her. "Go and rest."

Shooting him a scathing look, she rose to her feet, the noise of her silence deafening as she walked stiffly to the pile of soft furs in the corner. She huffed and tossed the furs back and forth, muttering what he was sure was steady stream of curses as she arranged the covers to her liking and lay down.

Dànel grabbed his quiver and leather pouch and returned to sit by the waning fire. Opening the leather pouch, he removed two soft goose feathers and ran the silky soft vane through his fingers before he laid them on a wooden board. His eyes drifted to where Ásta now lay wrapped in his furs with her back to him. All he could see was the very top of her head and the carved bone comb that she used to keep her fiery hair off her face, a comb just like the one his sister had worn. His chest tightened at the painful reminder of Tóra and he firmed his resolve—he would not lose another woman on his watch, never again.

"Are you just going to watch me, or are you coming to bed?" she snapped, somehow sensing his gaze.

Dànel sliced into a feather, preparing it for arrow fletching. "And get a welcome colder than a frozen fish in mid-winter? I think not. Go to sleep, Ásta."

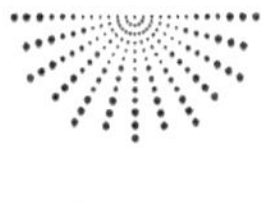

CHAPTER THREE

Ásta sat beside the fire stirring the elk stew with a carved wooden spoon as she caressed the rounded bump that had grown over the last few weeks. Her chest tightened as she tried and failed to make sense of the battle she fought within. Why was this so hard? She wanted to embrace this new child for the blessing it was, but her swollen stomach was a bittersweet reminder of all she had lost.

"Ásta, have you seen my other tunic?" Dànel said, interrupting her thoughts as he dug around noisily in the wooden chest in the corner.

"Look harder. It is in there." She sighed at the mess he was making of the clothing she'd neatly folded.

"Found it." He straightened, giving her a view of his broad shoulders and the lean lines of his back tapering in to where his breeches hung at his waist.

She blushed at the memory of what she knew those pants hid. His member was thick, long, and rock hard in the mornings when it poked her in the back. She'd been in the north a full moon now, and though they shared furs each night, Dànel had kept his word and not touched her. At first it had been a relief not to be tempted to betray her vow to Njal, but now she wondered if her changing body disgusted Dànel. He was a warrior in his prime, his body still young and virile, whereas she had recently begun to show signs of her age.

Dànel sat beside her and held the wooden bowls so she could serve the stew. "Would you like to come to the market today?"

"It would be lovely to get outside."

"I know it is hard to be inside all the time, but it is best not to go out in the cold."

"Já. All I want is to talk to somebody other than you, anyone but you."

Dànel chuckled. "Mayhap we have been too careful. I will come for you after the gathering." His expression darkened at the mention of the gathering to welcome the guests to the winter market.

"All will be well, Dànel." Without thinking Ásta reached out and patted his arm gently. She knew that the family of the woman he was supposed to marry was weighing on his mind, and she hated that she had caused him so much trouble.

"We shall see."

She offered him a weak smile. "I know you will negotiate a new deal and prove to the elders that you deserve your place as a leader."

"Mayhap...I will be glad when it is done."

Ásta gave him a reassuring smile. "Eat your food. You worry too much." It had not taken her long to realize that he was strong-minded and fair with a sharp wit that served him well when dealing with difficult people. He could fix the strained relations—he just lacked the confidence.

"The elders have cause to be concerned. I am not good at negotiation like my brother was," he said between spoonfuls of stew.

"Don't listen to them. You have lived a different life to your brother, so you have different skills. Use what you know to get what you want." She would not let him walk into that meeting feeling defeated when a little hint would give him the solution he needed.

"I want a deal," he snapped, placing the empty bowl in front of him. "But it is unlikely."

Ásta swallowed a mouthful of moose stew and feigned a casual offhandedness as she spoke. "It is true that reparations are necessary, however it is your ships that carry the wares to market. It seems to me that the power lies with you."

Brow furrowing, he crossed his powerful arms over his chest and considered her words.

Ásta cast him a sideways glance, then quickly bent over her food to hide her smile.

"I do have the only ships large enough to make the journey north. If Helmend Sidhault wants to trade he must deal with me."

"You said that the Sidhault family supplies the furs you need to trade with the Viking in the south."

"Já."

"Then you must be careful. It would be a great loss of coin and reputation to be unable to meet demand for such essential items." As she cleared away their bowls to the counter, she heard him rise behind her.

"That cannot happen," he said, lifting the pot of hot water from the fire and pouring it into the washing pan.

Ignoring the heat of him standing beside her, Ásta tested the temperature with her fingers then dipped the washcloth in. "Not all trades are done in meetings."

"What did you say?" Dànel looked at her sharply.

She shrugged, then wiped down a bowl and placed it on a cloth to dry. "Only that many trades are made outside of official gatherings."

His eyes narrowed as the meaning behind her words registered.

Carefully washing the carved wooden spoons, she set them aside. She had planted the seed, now the rest was on him.

"I must find Helmend Sidhault at once."

A wry half smile curved her lips as she watched him cross to the door in three strides. He learnt fast. Dirty dishes forgotten, she leaned back against the counter thankful for the support as she watched his firm ass cheeks flex as he bent at the waist to pull on his boots.

He spun around to face her. "My thanks, Ásta," he said, as he hastily wrapped his fur cloak around his shoulders and fastened the silver clasp.

She waved him off. "Hurry. Go now."

Dànel nodded and unlatched the door. "I will come for you later."

~

The eerie twilight haze had faded into the darkness long before Ásta heard Dànel stomp the snow off his boots outside the door. She didn't know why he bothered since it made little difference to the constant puddles of water he left inside the doorway.

The door opened and he poked his head inside. "Shall we go?"

"I just need my fur," she said, having pulled on her boots when she'd heard his footsteps crunching in the snow outside. She walked toward where he stood, his broad shoulders blocking all view of the outside. As the distance between them narrowed, her skin heated with unsettling warmth.

"How was your day?" he asked, standing so close that her breath caught as he wrapped the soft fur of a brown bear around her shoulders and fastened it.

Ásta quelled the surge of tenderness she felt when Dànel treated her with the affection of a man caring for his woman.

How long had it been since she was loved in this way? Njal had loved her with such devotion. But Dànel was… She silently cursed herself. This wasn't Njal—it was wrong to feel anything for another man.

"I spent the day mending. Tell me, how do you put so many holes in your clothes?"

Dànel's face split into a wide grin. "It is a gift."

Her heart skipped at that boyish smile that had won her over last time. "Mayhap you should add mending to your chores? Soon I shall be too busy to keep up."

He moved aside so she could pass. "I promise to be more careful. Did you eat?"

"Not yet. I fell asleep." She stepped out into the frigid night, breathing in the sweet fresh scent of the pine forest that Dànel had told her reached the far northern mountains and then beyond to the frozen glaciers of the tundra.

Dànel fastened the latch on the door and joined her. "The noaidi says you are tired because the baby takes the life from you and uses it to grow."

"You should stop talking to the shaman about me." A smiled tugged at the corners of her mouth as she pulled her fur hat down over her ears to keep the snow off her head.

"He knows of such things." Dànel grinned at her, and for a moment, she saw the playful man that wooed her at Valen's wedding.

Arching a brow, she studied him intently. Her stomach fluttered. He had told her that the shaman was only ever consulted for those you cared for. She stomped her feet to ward against the cold as the guilt crept in. Was it so wrong to feel pleasure from knowing he cared about her? Was she betraying Njal? Her heart. Óðinn help her, it felt like she'd never sort through her feelings or the questions that had plagued her since his death.

"Are you avoiding telling me about what happened today because it is bad news?"

Dànel smirked. "I wondered how long it would take you to ask."

"Stop teasing." Ásta shoved him playfully, hitting a wall of solid muscle that refused to move.

A smug expression crossed his face. "Come. Let's get some food and I'll tell you." Linking her arm through his, Dànel led her along the trail toward the marketplace, seemingly unaffected by her proximity as he told her of the successful negotiation with Helmend and the shock on his uncle's face when he'd announced it at the gathering.

Ásta struggled to ignore the brush of his taut muscular limbs against hers and the desire pooling between her legs.

"Once I had the Sidhault agreement, the others were eager to trade too," he said proudly, oblivious to her plight.

"So the elders were pleased?"

Wrapping an arm around her waist, he pulled her closer and ushered her through the market, using his body to shield her from the crowd.

"I believe so. I secured all we need to satisfy the agreements with the Isaksson and Eriksson clans."

Ásta was so caught up in the pleasure of being cocooned in the arms of a man once more that she almost forgot to reply. "I am glad, Dànel. I knew you could do it."

Halting in the midst of the bustling crowd, Dànel looked down at her, his expression serious. "You gave me the idea, Ásta. I'm not good at politics like Ándde was."

In the dim light of the torches that lined the market stalls, the shadow of his dark stubble sharpened the lines of his angular jaw as his eyes conveyed his thanks and something more powerful.

A lump rose in her throat as his eyes relayed his message—he saw her, truly saw her as a woman with the smarts to match any man. Tears formed in her eyes, for it had been many years since anyone had looked at her like that.

"It was you that made the deal. You are already a strong leader."

Dànel's nostrils flared, his eyes glowing with hunger and lust. Then he grabbed her hand and pulled her behind a stall selling wolf and beaver furs.

She looked up at him in surprise. What was he doing?

"Ásta," he said in a ragged whisper, then his gaze fell to her lips and darkened to the unmistakable smoulder of a man fighting to hold himself back.

Heat flushed her skin. By the gods, when he looked at her like she was a delicious sweet treat she wanted to surrender and lose herself in him.

Time stopped as the flaming torch behind him flickered across his ruggedly handsome face, everything disappearing as the air crackled with the carnal promise between them.

Bending, he moved closer ever so slowly, until she could feel his breath warming her cheek as his lips hovered over hers.

Their breath mingled into a warm cloud that hit the crisp night air, then floated away on a breeze, taking with it her will to resist her yearning for this man. Her nipples pebbled against the coarse fabric of her dress. Blessed Freya, she wanted him, now.

When his lips brushed across hers, the tender touch conveyed his desire yet still sought permission. He was holding back, but she needed more. She wanted to feel him plunder her mouth and lose control.

Before she could stop herself, Ásta stepped closer and melted against him, her hands clutching his shoulders as she opened her mouth and allowed him in.

Growling in approval, he wrapped her in his arms, one hand cradling the back of her head as he deepened the kiss. His mouth moved earnestly, nipping and coaxing until her heart raced and she lost all reason but the yen for more.

"Gods, Ásta." His hand slid down her back, and then around

to her front, and slipped beneath her fur cloak. The heat of his breath warmed her neck as his hand cupped her breast, weighing it gently in his palm before his thumb brushed across her nipple.

Startled, her body stiffened. What was she doing? Her body was betraying her, but her heart belonged to another. Somehow, she found the will to put a hand on his chest and push him back, instantly feeling bereft at the loss of his touch.

"Nei. I cannot." She would not do this to Dànel. He deserved a woman that could give him her whole heart, not someone haunted by a lost love.

Dànel stepped back and studied her thoughtfully.

The question in his gaze stripped her bare, leaving her feeling vulnerable and exposed. Dànel could see far too much of her broken and battered heart, but she saw none of the judgement she'd expected from him. Instead, she saw both understanding and a tender resolve to win her over. Too bad. He would be sorely disappointed.

The air between them cooled as fast as the hunger in his eyes, then he nodded once and turned back toward the market.

"Come. Let's get you fed and go listen to the yoiking."

A short while and one steaming bowl of reindeer stew later, Ásta stood inspecting an array of wooden cups, leather pouches, and every manner of fur conceivable, whilst trying not to have every nerve aware of the man beside her. She traced a finger over the carved bone handle of a dagger admiringly, before a small wooden sled caught her eye.

Dànel continued talking with the stallholder.

How could he act so nonchalant when her whole body was aflame?

"Are you ready to hear the singing?"

Ásta tore her gaze from the small wooden sled, banishing the image of Dànel pulling their laughing child through the snow from her mind.

Dànel glanced at the sled, and then back at her before he raised an eyebrow questioningly.

She looked away to hide the blush that she knew would turn her pale skin as dark as lingonberry jam. Gods, could she hide nothing from him?

"Let's go then, little mumma."

A lump formed in her throat at the tender endearment. Was he trying to win her over with affection?

Grabbing her gloved hand, Dànel led her toward the sweet melody that drifted on the night air like a woodlark singing in the summer sun. The woman's voice rose into one last soaring note and then ebbed just they came to a stop near a roaring bonfire.

Ásta stepped closer to the flames and sighed as warmth blew across her nose. She hadn't realized how cold she had become in the short time they had been at the market.

Putting his arms around her shoulders, Dànel pulled her into his chest.

She stiffened as his arms wrapped around her. "What are you doing?"

"Keeping you warm," he said, and began to speak with the man beside him, his indifference making it clear that he was offering her warmth, not more temptation.

She relaxed, not entirely sure if she was relieved or disappointed that she could accept this warm embrace from him without it meaning more. Resting her head on the thick fur covering his chest, she let her eyes drift closed and her fingers slide through the softness, tracing the hard planes of his chest beneath.

A few moments later, the chattering crowd around them fell silent and the deep cadence of a mournful song filled the air.

Though there were no words, the man's dulcet tone swept Ásta along on his journey. Her heart sang and then bled as she shared every moment of his joy and anguish in the emotion-laden song. A tear ran down her cheek as the haunting final note rang through the night, leaving her filled with a hopefulness that defied reason. *What was this magic?* she wondered, vaguely aware of the noise of the crowd shifting around her as the mesmerizing trance ended.

"Ásta?" Dànel squeezed her shoulder gently.

She opened her eyes to search for the singer. She wanted to meet him, to ask what had inspired such beauty.

"You never mentioned the magic of the yoik, Dànel." Rising up on her toes, Ásta peered over the small crowd gathered to congratulate the performer. "Why have I never heard a yoik at court?"

"The Sámi do not stray far from the north."

A mass of brown fur and a set of furious dark eyes caught her attention. Instantly, the fetid tang of bile rose in her throat and her whole body tingled as though she had been struck by lightning.

The man stood stationary in the moving crowd, watching her.

Nei! She slapped her hand over her mouth and swallowed hard to keep from losing her dinner. Her chest tightened until it was difficult to breathe.

Mattias! He'd found her.

Her skin crawled and a shiver crept up her spine as his green eyes slithered over her. It felt like he was trying to strip her bare and violate her with his eyes. Her heartbeat sounded like a hollow drum thundering in her ears.

Then he smirked like a hunter who knew he'd cornered his prey and a strangled cry escaped her lips.

She needed to run, *now.*

CHAPTER FOUR

DÁNEL

"Ásta, are you well?" Dànel asked, looking down at her ashen face.

She ignored him, her eyes remaining fixed on something in the distance.

He followed her gaze to where a large man in brown bear fur stood returning her stare with an intensity that had his hand falling to the sword at his waist.

The high-pitched squeak of her voice was unrecognisable when Ásta finally spoke.

"He's here. Mattias is here."

Dànel's fingers tightened on the well-worn hilt of his blade, but his eyes never left King Mattias of Jottland. He studied the man carefully, searching for weakness. The King was taller than he remembered from their brief meeting at Valen's wedding, with thick dark hair that hung low over his sinister eyes and a matching beard that obscured the lower half of his face and jaw.

Dànel's jaw clenched. Mattias' gaze remained fixed on Ásta with a wild fervor that he had seen before, in the eyes of men whose minds dwelt far beyond reason. Dànel stepped in front of

Ásta, shielding her from view. He would *never* let the man anywhere near her.

King Mattias crossed his arms over his chest, his assessing gaze slowly moving upward to meet those of the man that held what he coveted.

Slowly cracking his neck back and forth, Daniel held his gaze and let his mouth form the mirthless smirk he knew would stoke the King's rage. He'd offer this man no mercy and feel no remorse when he cut him down.

The king's dark brows furrowed in response, then his eyes blazed with a look deliberately intended to strike fear.

Dànel widened his smile, his eyes shooting some icy daggers of their own. That look might make others cower, but he knew Vikings—they were his brothers. He'd faced berserkers far more terrifying than this well-fed King who sent men out to die while he watched the battle unfold from the safety of camp. Now that he had the coward King's attention, it was time to issue the dare. He knew how men like Mattias worked—they thought the victory was theirs before the battle had begun, but this was his land and nobody would best him in this terrain. All he needed to do was bait Mattias to the battlefield.

Dànel turned and pulled Ásta into his arms. "Ásta, look at me," he demanded.

Her whole body trembled, but her eyes lifted to meet his.

"You are safe. Do you trust me?"

Her head bobbed in agreement, but the action lacked conviction. It would have to do for now—there was no time to convince her. He had to lure the King away from his home to keep his people safe.

Dipping his head, he pressed his mouth to hers, his tongue tracing the soft fullness of her lips until she opened for him. The moment he tasted her sweetness, he wrapped his arms around her and deepened the kiss, forgetting that he'd kissed her merely to announce his claim on her to their audience.

She moaned softly as he took her mouth with a savage intensity, surrendering to the pleasure.

She belonged with him. Nobody was taking her away. Brushing his lips across hers one final time, he pulled back, still holding her close as his attention returned to the enemy.

The King's top lip curled into an ugly snarl, then he turned and barked an order to the warrior standing behind him.

Without hesitating, Dànel swept Ásta's feet out from under her and held her in his arms. "Karl, I need a full guard, *now*," he ordered the man at his side.

His old friend snapped to attention and waved a hand overhead to signal others. "What is it?"

"She is in danger." He nodded at the King. "Send men to watch him and his men. Do not let any of them out of sight."

Moments later, Dànel carried Ásta through the market flanked by eight of his ship's crew. They must make haste. Mattias would soon come for her. It was not safe here.

"Karl. Saddle Tyr with supplies and put a full guard around the hut."

"Já. Do not worry—nobody will get through, brother."

Satisfied that they were safe for now, he stepped inside his hut and lowered Ásta to the ground.

She was shaking so hard that he could hear her teeth chattering, but she stumbled to the pile of furs and lay down, her body curling into a tight ball.

"Ásta. You must get up."

He bent over and shook her shoulder gently.

"We have to leave. You need to pack the bags."

She rolled over, her glazed eyes looking straight through him.

Hel! He ran a hand through his hair. She was so terrified that she'd disappeared inside herself. He couldn't take her anywhere like this. He needed to bring her back, *now*.

"Ásta," he barked, as though scolding a naughty child.

She blinked, her pale lashes opening. "Dànel?" Her voice was a hoarse whisper.

"I'm here." He rubbed her shoulder. "You need to pack."

"We're leaving?" Her body uncoiled and she clumsily pushed herself upright.

He crouched down in front of her and offered a comforting smile. "Já. We must leave, quickly."

She shook her head back and forth as her panicked eyes filled with tears. "He'll find us. He always does."

"Look at me, Ásta." When she met his gaze, he continued. "Nobody can hide in this land like my people. He will never find you. I promise." He offered her his hand and waited for her response. "I will protect you, but I need you to trust me. Can you do that?"

Ásta swallowed hard, and then placed her hand in his.

After pulling her to her feet and making sure she was steady, he pointed to the leather bags he used when he went raiding.

"Pack all we will need for a long journey."

Gathering herself, she nodded, her tear-stained face the only sign of her earlier terror. "I can do that."

Dànel tucked a lock of hair behind her ear. He was proud of her—her delicate exterior hid a fierce warrior within. He let his fingers slide down the long lean line of her neck, feeling the quickening of her pulse beneath her alabaster skin.

Her breath caught.

He closed the space between them, almost groaning at the sensation of her body pressed to his. He hardened. *Óðinn!* It was entirely the wrong time for his cock to misbehave.

"I trust you, Dànel," she said, and then her tongue slid across her lips slowly, beckoning him.

He had to taste her again. Unable to stop himself, Dànel leaned in and their lips met in a lingering, savoring kiss.

Ásta released a soft throaty moan and softened against him.

He nipped and sucked at her bottom lip, scraping his teeth

across the tender flesh before he pulled away. They could not do this now, but this was *far* from finished.

"We must go. Pack the bags," he said, and left her standing there looking slightly stunned.

After leaving orders for his men and checking on his stallion, Dànel hurried back to Ásta. With any luck, they'd be on the trail long before Mattias could ready his men.

"Dànel? You are leaving. What has happened?"

Sighing heavily, he spun around to face his Aunt Tuá. His father's sister would not be pleased that he was running out on his duties to the siida. She had been cautiously welcoming of his return, but he knew that she was not yet convinced he deserved to lead.

"There is a dangerous man threatening Ásta."

The wrinkles in his aunt's brow deepened as she frowned. "Where are you going?"

Dànel steeled himself for the onslaught of her temper. She would not like this, but there was naught he could do.

"To the summer lands."

Her eyes widened and she stumbled backward. "Nei. You cannot take the girl there. Winter will soon set in. You know how dangerous it is."

A hard lump formed in his gut. How could he forget? It was he who had watched his sister disappear below the ice, he who had lived with the guilt and blame every day since.

"You think I want this? I know the risk better than any."

"But what happened with Tóra..."

Nei! He couldn't bear to hear talk of Tóra, not when he was taking Ásta, who knew even less of how to survive on the land, out into the same wilderness that had stolen his sister.

"Do not speak of Tóra." Icy dread filled him at the thought of a similar fate befalling Ásta, but he had little choice. "This is the only way to keep Ásta safe."

"Who is this threat? We can fight. We can protect her if you stay."

Shaking his head, Dànel wished that she were right. "This is not a battle that can be won here." He would not watch his kin fall to Viking steel. "We must draw him away from the siida."

His aunt's beady eyes studied him thoughtfully for a few moments. "Very well, nephew. Be sure to listen to the call of the land."

CHAPTER FIVE

ÁSTA

*Á*sta stomped her foot and glared at where Dànel stood beside his stallion impatiently waiting to hoist her back onto his mount.

"I am not getting back on," she said in a stern tone that conveyed her conviction. She meant it. They'd barely stopped in two days, except to water and feed themselves and the horse, and for her to relieve her aching bladder. She'd had enough. She'd even slept on the stallion when Dànel insisted they ride through the night. Did the man ever sleep?

Dànel tied the reins around a tree and patted Tyr on his sweaty round rump.

At first, she'd been terrified of the stallion with the wind-blown curly mane, long tail, and glossy coat as dark as the night sky. He looked like a beast escaped from Hel's underworld. But these last few days she had come to adore the powerful creature that was nimble, even-tempered, and devoted to Dànel.

Dànel crossed his arms over his chest, a sure sign that he was about to attempt to bend her to his will.

"We need to keep moving. Tyr can go a while longer."

She glared at him defiantly. "I cannot." This time he would

not win. She was a calm and patient woman, but he had pushed her to the end of her tether. Her whole body ached as she stomped over to him, especially her thighs and lower back.

"No more riding until I have slept." She poked him in the chest as she spoke through clenched teeth.

A muscle in his jaw ticked as he looked down at her prodding finger, then back up at her. "We will camp here for the night," he said, as though it was his plan all along, "and leave at first light."

Huffing in exasperation, Ásta turned on her heel and shuffled stiffly away from him. *Infuriating. Foolish. Boneheaded.* Muttering increasingly colorful expletives, she walked around the edge of the small clearing in the thick snow-laden forest, hoping to ease her cramping legs.

"Don't wander off," Dànel said a short while later, after he had finished unloading the supplies from Tyr.

She turned to face him, noting the dark shadows under his eyes. He was not as unaffected by the lack of sleep as he'd have her think.

"You can start the fire while I cut poles for the lávvu."

"The what?"

"The lávvu, the tent."

"Oh. A warm tent sounds wonderful."

"Good. You make the fire." Dànel pulled a small axe from one of the bags he'd left leaning against a tree and then walked toward the forest.

"Dànel?"

He paused and looked back over a shoulder at her. "Já."

"I don't know how to light a fire."

"What?" His brow furrowed in disbelief. "How can you not know how to make a fire?"

Ásta bristled at the accusation in his voice. "My father was a king. We had servants for such things. I would have been scolded if I even attempted to do it myself."

"But it is a handmaiden's task."

"Rúna insisted I never do it. She had the other women light the fire in her chamber."

Dànel pursed his lips and shook his head disapprovingly. "Then you shall learn."

Ásta paced back and forth, her ire growing as Dànel wandered through the undergrowth collecting sticks and then pulled a few logs from his saddlebag. How dare he scoff at her inability to perform a task forbidden to her? Could he entertain a room full of nobles, or embroider an intricate design? She'd bet not.

Daniel dropped a pile of wood in a heap and placed stones in a small circle, then squatted down and placed the axe beside him.

"Come," he said, and motioned her forward.

"I shall watch you do it."

He shook his head. "Nei. To learn, you must do."

"But—"

"No arguing, Ásta." He continued talking, unaware of her rising indignation. "You must learn to do it. You will need fire to survive when I leave you at the hut alone."

Entirely too weary to fight common sense, Ásta made her way over to him.

"First you need some Birchwood shavings." Dànel opened a small leather pouch on his belt and dipped his hand inside. Then he placed a large handful of wood shavings in the stone circle and retied the pouch. "I'll show you how to cut them another day. You cannot make fire without it, so you must never run out."

Ásta nodded wearily. "Birchwood shavings. That seems simple."

"Next you break the twigs into smaller pieces like this"— Dànel's corded hands flexed as he snapped a branch in half in demonstration—"so that they are ready to go on the fire. Do you see?"

"Já."

Grabbing his axe, he stood upright and motioned at the pile of wood he'd collected. "Good. You finish breaking the wood. I will cut the poles we need," he said, and strode off.

A short while later, Ásta hissed and threw the last of the broken sticks at her feet. Her fingers were numb because she'd had to remove her cumbersome fur gloves to complete the task, and her palms hurt where the bark had rubbed her skin raw.

Dànel lumbered casually into view carrying fresh cut lengths of birch over his shoulder. "Are you finished?" he asked as he placed them on the ground.

"Já. It is done."

Ásta blew on her fingers and then pulled her gloves back on.

"Good." Kneeling beside her, Dànel began to place wood on the pile of shavings.

Ásta bit back a sharp retort. He could have at least shown some appreciation for her hard work. She kicked the snow away until the earth was bare, and then sat on the ground beside him.

"What now?"

She watched as he pulled an old worn leather pouch from his pocket and tipped the contents into his hand.

"This is a fire steel." He slid three fingers through a curved piece of steel and held it up for her to see. Then he placed a small rock and a piece of something brown on one of the flat stones surrounding the fire. "That is horseshoe fungus and a flint stone."

A what? Ásta nodded, pretending she knew what it was.

"You hold the shavings in your hand, place the fungus on top, and then strike the flint across the fire steel downward like this." Sparks flew when he struck the steel with the small piece of rock repeatedly in a fast fluid motion.

Now that she'd seen him do it, Ásta recalled seeing her own handmaidens complete this task. She'd just never paid it much attention.

"When the sparks hit the birch shavings they will begin to smoke and you can place them in the fire pit and add the smallest twigs, slanting them upright."

He pulled the fire steel off his hand and held it out to her with the flint stone.

"Now you do it, while I put up the tent."

~

sta winced and looked down at her swollen and bruised thumb. Dànel had almost finished constructing the tent around her and she had yet to make a single spark. Was this one of Loki's tricks?

"I cannot do this."

"You can," Dànel said, pulling the hide covering over the last of the poles, completely sealing off the outside.

Ásta grit her teeth and struck the steel with the flint once more. This time the sharp rock slid off to the side and scraped across her knuckles, drawing blood.

"That is it. I am *not* doing this anymore," she snapped, throwing the fire steel and flint to the ground and rising to her feet. "If you want a fire, make your own."

The reindeer hide tent flap lifted and Dànel walked over to stand beside her. "You must do this," he insisted, a frown marring his handsome features as he looked down at the lopsided pile of sticks she had built.

"I. Will. Not." She gave him a scathing look.

He huffed once in disgust, and then ignored her as he lit the shavings in three strikes and then built the fire over them. Once he'd place a larger log on the top, he rose to his feet.

"I'll not do this for you again, Ásta. You must practice until you can do it for yourself."

Her face burned as his words hit her in the chest. How dare he speak to her like that? "Do not scold me like a disobedient child. Mayhap I need a better teacher?" she taunted.

Dànel's jaw ticked, but he ignored her jibe and crossed to the tent opening.

"I shall feed and retire Tyr for the night. At least try to keep the fire lit."

Her eyes filled with tears, guilt settling heavy in her gut as she watched him disappear. She didn't want to feel like this anymore, like a boat set adrift to the mercy of the tides of life and chance. What had she been thinking coming here? She would never be brave like Rúna, or able to make fires and butcher animals. She was a queen, not a warrior.

CHAPTER SIX

DÁNEL

ànel struck the flint and blew gently on the small pile of tinder until the flames lit every corner of the reindeer hide tent.

"Where is she?" Ásta had left a while ago to relieve herself and should be back by now. "Stubborn woman." For the last three days, she had delayed lighting a fire with all manner of excuses until he was forced to take over the task. It had to stop —her childish tantrum was putting her at risk. How in Hel did she expect to survive in the north if she couldn't master the simplest of tasks? Cursing under his breath, he tossed more logs on the fire and rose to his feet.

Pushing back the tent flap, he called out to her and stepped out into the moonless dusk that heralded a bitterly cold night ahead.

Silence.

"Ásta?"

Tyr shuffled, his hooves crunching in the snow as he noisily devoured his feed.

"Ásta?" he called a little louder. Where in Hel was she? He

walked around the tent, scanning the forest, but the snow-covered foliage was too thick to see very far.

"Ásta!" he shouted, his throat constricting when she still did not reply. Had Mattias taken her? Or had she wandered off?

A cold knot formed in his gut. Fighting down his rising panic, he slowed his pace and skirted along the tree line, searching the forest floor and undergrowth for signs of her trail. He had to find her before darkness fell—wolves roamed this forest along with more than a few large bears. His heart raced as the all too familiar fear crept in.

"Tóra..." Her name fell from his lips in a pained whisper as the memories flooded back. His sister had been his responsibility and he'd failed her.

"Not this time," he muttered. "Not again."

Spotting a broken branch that must have snapped as Ásta walked past, Dànel jogged along the well-worn animal trail hoping that Ásta had not encountered a predator on the hunt.

It was almost entirely dark when he spotted her hiding behind a large pine watching a small deer ambling through the snow.

A sigh of relief escaped him as he hurried toward her. Thank Óðinn, she was unharmed.

He'd told her not to wander off. What had she been thinking? She could have been killed. With every step he took, his anger rose until his steaming breath was but a small indication of the impending eruption he struggled to restrain.

"Ásta," he yelled when she rounded the tree trunk and disappeared from view. She was not getting away from him again. Not while he still breathed. He would march her back to camp and tie her up if that was what it would take to keep her safe.

"Over here."

Dànel stomped towards her. The foolish woman had wandered off into the forest alone, without a weapon *and* away from the track.

"What in Hel are you doing?" he said as he approached, snow crunching beneath his boots.

"You scared it off," she accused, spinning around to glare at him.

Dànel halted in front of her, so close that he saw the moment her anger melted away and her eyes became wary. Placing his hands either side of her head on the tree trunk, he leaned in, his eyes pinning her with the full force of his fury.

"I told you not to leave camp," he ground out.

She stared up at him, her eyes lit with a flash of defiance. "It was but a short walk to stretch my legs."

"You could have been killed." He was shouting now. Astounded at her lack of self-preservation and that she was brazen enough to defend her foolishness.

"Don't be so ill-tempered. All is well."

"All is *not* well," he hissed.

"It is not?"

"Nei. You should be spanked like the insolent child you are."

Ásta recoiled in shock at his words, the back of her head hitting the tree trunk with a thud.

Dànel continued, determined to frighten the impertinence and daring fair out of this fearless queen. "Mayhap I should leave you to the wolves, bears, and lynx that hunt in this forest?"

Ásta's face blanched and she looked around. "I didn't—"

"You didn't *think*," he interrupted her. He leaned in, speaking in the deadly calm tone he used when scolding the men under his command. "You put yourself, and our baby, in danger. This pampered queen act is beneath you, Ásta. Grow up, and learn how to take care of yourself or despite my *every* effort, you *are* going die out here."

Her face paled as his words sunk in.

Good. It was long past time she understood the danger of her situation. There was no comfortable life in the north—she was in the wilds and would have to fight for survival like every-body else. The sooner she realized that the better.

A wolf's howl echoed in the distance.

Eyes widening in fear, Ásta swayed unsteadily.

Dànel threw up his hands. "See, out here you are food, just like every other animal. So, when I tell you not to wander off"—he slammed his hand against the tree to punctuate each word—"do-not-wander-off." Then, fighting back the urge to throw her over his shoulder, he spun around and stormed toward camp.

~

ÁSTA

Ásta sat in the warm tent across from Dànel wishing that he'd simply shout some more and be done with it, but his stony silence was absolute. For hours now, she had watched the firelight flicker across his somber features as he stared into the flames.

"Dànel, I am truly sorry for leaving camp."

Ignoring her, he continued to tear chunks of meat from the hare he'd roasted as soon as they'd returned to camp.

"Why can't you forgive me? I have apologized many times."

"You merely say what you think I wish to hear."

"That is not true."

Ásta studied the rigidness of his back and shoulders and the grim line on his lips.

"Why are you so angry?" All she had done was take a short walk. True, there were dangerous predators in this forest, but she had not known that at the time. Besides, she was perfectly well, until he'd come along and scared her out of her wits.

"I know I made a mistake, but it does not warrant such anger." Unless what happened earlier was not the problem.

Mayhap he was angry about the strife that had plagued him since her arrival? Had he decided she was more trouble than she was worth?

"I am sorry for bringing my problems to you. It was not fair."

Dànel met her entreating gaze, but the depths of his dark eyes betrayed no response.

Biting her lip, she refused to buckle under his intense stare. "I put your family in danger. I understand if you must abandon me." She dropped her eyes, unable to bear the weight of her own disappointment in herself. Coming here was the selfish act of a frightened child. A true queen, the person she had once been, would have sacrificed herself for the good of her people in a heartbeat. How had she strayed so far from who she was?

"You're not going anywhere."

She rushed on, not hearing his response. "It is for the best. I would do the same. You cannot risk many lives to save one."

"Two." His tone was harsh.

Her head snapped up. "What?"

"There are two lives." Dànel pointed the thighbone in his hand at her stomach.

She glanced down, then back up into his eyes. "Two lives for many is not a fair trade. I have put you in an impossible situation."

He tossed the bone into the fire. "That is not why I am angry."

"It's not?"

"Nei." Expression darkening, he averted his gaze. What was he keeping from her?

"Then why?"

"How long has it been since your husband died?"

She baulked and did not answer. Why would he ask her that?

He pinned her with an intent stare that made her uncomfortable. "Four years, is it? You need to move on."

"Don't tell me what I need."

Dànel sighed, his voice gentler when he spoke again. "You use your grief to shield yourself from life and the world around you, Ásta. Rúna may have allowed it, but I will not. It has to stop. Gods woman, you put yourself in danger to follow a blasted deer."

"I am perfectly well," she said through clenched teeth. Is that what he truly thought of her? That she was using Njal as an excuse not to live, to walk though life unaware? Was she?

"Stop behaving like a pampered queen and start thinking about the child you carry."

Even as she recoiled from the force of his words, Dànel continued. "There are no kings and queens out here, Ásta. We all are equal on this land. It is our skills that help us to conquer and survive."

"I've tried to light the fire—"

"Nei,' he snapped, cutting her off. "You failed once, then gave up. You can't even follow simple instructions to stay close to camp." He ran his hand through his hair, his frustration evident. "This is no place for whimsy and wandering off, Ásta. People die out here."

And there it was, the inkling she knew would lead to the root cause of his anger.

"*People* die out here?" she repeated.

"Já. One mistake and you could be one of them."

She watched him hesitate, and then his voice hardened with a guilt that she knew could only be caused by years and years of layered regret.

"My own sister died in these woods."

Her breath stilled for a moment. "She did?"

Pain flashed across his face as she waited for him to explain. "Mother sent us out to collect firewood, wanting us out from underfoot whilst she worked. She trusted me to care for Tóra."

"You were a good brother."

"Not that day." Dànel gazed into the fire, the orange flames doing little to warm his haunted eyes. "I put some branches beside the trail to collect on our way home, and when I turned back..."

A chill swept over Ásta.

His voice cracked. 'She was gone."

"She wandered off," Ásta whispered, everything finally making sense to her.

Clearing his throat, Dànel poked at the fire with a stick. When he continued, his words were stilted and hollow, and it was clear that he was recounting memories as they flashed though his mind.

"She was at the river, playing on the ice. I called out to warn her it was dangerous, but she ran away. It was a game we played —her running, me chasing."

He blames himself. "You were but children."

Dànel ignored her attempt to placate his guilt. "The ice had melted early that year—it cracked beneath her feet. She...fell into the water."

Ásta closed her eyes, not wanting him to see the pity there, and let the tears pool beneath her lashes. Curse the cruel gods for thrusting such horror on a young boy!

"What did you do?" she asked, looking at him.

Pain and sorrow etched his face, making him look older than his years. "I crawled out to the edge, but she was gone, swept downstream, trapped beneath the ice."

"I am so sorry, Dànel."

His brows furrowed and she was silenced by his dark angry expression. "I don't want your pity, Ásta. I told you so that you would understand the danger you put yourself in."

"I understand now. I am sorry."

The silence stretched between them as he searched her face. "I believe you," he said, and leaned back on his hands, stretching his long legs out before him. "I was at fault, too. That is why I was angry. You would never have wandered off if I had made you see how dangerous it is out here."

"I will try harder," Ásta said, silently vowing not to add another two deaths to his tally of guilt and regret. She would learn how to survive in this wild land, for him, herself, and their baby. "I will not give up this time. I promise."

CHAPTER SEVEN

*D*ánel watched Ásta carefully make her way back along the narrow animal trail that led to the stream. Collecting water from the small trickle that had not yet frozen over was a welcome change to melting snow over the fire to quench their thirst and satisfy Tyr's needs too.

Ásta held the tanned hide water pouch in her right hand, her shuffling stiff gait far from her usual smooth glide. She brushed a handful of sweat-dampened hair off her face. It had been four days since their fight and the dark circles under her eyes betrayed her fatigue, yet when she saw him, she thrust her stooped shoulders back and hastened to where he waited.

Warmth flooded his chest at the sight of her seeking to impress him. She had kept her promise to not give up, listening intently to everything he had taught her over the last few days. After they made camp this afternoon, he had finally challenged her to put his lessons to use with this simple task.

"I got it." Ásta halted in front of him, panting heavily as she held up the water pouch triumphantly.

"Good. I see you remembered to layer in warm clothing. Did you take the fire steel and flint?"

She pulled them from her pocket and held them up triumphantly.

"Very good. Never go anywhere without the tools to make fire. Did you stay on the trail?"

She nodded. "I stopped often to listen for animals too."

Dànel smiled approvingly. At least her earlier mistake had made her aware of the predators that roamed the forest. "And you have the knife?"

"Já. Always carry a weapon on your body." She repeated his words back to him.

His smile widened as unexpected warmth filled his chest. But as he took the water from her hand, he noticed the soft brown leather of her boots was damp and icy crystals had formed over the wet laces.

"Your boots are wet."

"It is naught. I slipped on a rock."

As Ásta waved off his concern, Dànel realized he'd forgotten one important lesson. "It is not naught, Ásta. Getting wet is very dangerous in this cold. It can kill a person in minutes."

Ásta looked down at the cause of her failure. "It is just my boots."

"Wet boots can lead to losing toes or even a foot. You must stay dry at all times."

Ásta's brow furrowed, and when she lifted her eyes her disappointment was evident.

"You did well."

Shrugging off his reassurance, she looked down at her feet dejectedly.

He was glad she was taking this seriously, but she was being too hard on herself. Cupping her chin with his hand, he gently lifted until her eyes met his. "I am proud of you. It was my fault. There is no shame in failing a lesson not taught," he insisted.

His blood heated, the air between them becoming thick and heady as his thumb gently caressed her cheek. Resisting the urge to touch her was becoming harder with each passing day. Gods, he had never wanted anything more than to feel her beneath him again. Without thinking he asked the question that had been plaguing him.

"Why did you let me into your bed, Ásta?"

Her breath caught and she paled. "I—I don't know." It was a lie and they both knew it.

"You do. Tell me."

"I was lonely," she whispered, avoiding his gaze.

Letting his hand fall away, he studied her thoughtfully, then shook his head. "Nei. That is not why." If it were loneliness, she would have taken a lover long before he came along.

"Do not pretend that that night was just a casual encounter. I've never wanted a woman more, and I know you wanted me too."

A blush crept into her cheeks. "Don't do this," she whispered, pulling away.

Dànel lowered his voice and spoke slowly, decisively, so she could not doubt his resolve. "I *still* want you, *all* of you, but I'll not have another man in our bed."

Moving aside, he nodded for her to continue back to camp. "One day you will admit that that is what you want, too. Now, go warm your feet. I will collect more wood."

~

ÁSTA

*T*wo days later, Ásta cursed under her breath and struck the flint against the fire steel.

"I *will* do this."

She struck again. She was done with failing. This eve she would light the cursed fire before Dànel got back and had to do it for her, again.

"That is not happening!" Even if her knuckles bled, she would do it. Sucking in a fortifying breath, she straightened her shoulders and firmed her resolve. She couldn't hold the fungus and strike the steel without fumbling, so she placed some wood shavings and the brown piece of fungus on a flat rock instead.

"I *will* do this."

The flint rock screeched as it struck the fire steel, and again, and again.

Before long, her fingers burned, but she refused to admit defeat. There was naught she could do as Njal was cut down in front of her, nor as the precious life was torn from her body that day. And her four summers with Rúna had been ruled by inaction and fear, but she was done with that.

"I *will* light this cursed fire that will protect you," she promised her baby. "Or I will kill myself trying." Her breath hitched as a spark flew and landed on the fungus. She struck three more times.

A wisp of smoke curled up and danced in front of her eyes.

Her heart leapt to her throat. She placed some more shavings on top as she'd seen Dànel do, and then blew gently.

A tiny flame burst to life.

Her heart raced as she lifted the smouldering fungus into the fire circle, added more shavings, and watched the fire crackle as the flames devoured the dry woodchips.

It was working! She added a handful of the smallest twigs, and then larger and larger ones when they caught alight.

Finally, when the flames danced high and the heat was too much to bear, she sat back on her haunches and watched the orange and red glow, satisfaction warming her heart.

"I did it," she whispered. She'd made a fire.

Just then, Dànel entered the tent carrying a wild duck in one hand and his bow and quiver in the other.

"Look," she exclaimed, grinning up at him. "I lit the fire."

"Well done, Ásta." He placed the duck on the counter and

crouched down beside her to inspect her work. "You can add some of the larger pieces now." He smiled at her.

"It is a good fire, já?"

"Já. It will burn all night." His smile broadened, and when his eyes crinkled in the corners, she was reminded of the jovial man he'd been when they'd first met. Clearly her mastering the fire lighting and other skills he insisted she learn had taken a weight off his shoulders. She was glad for that.

"I cannot believe I did it."

"I knew you would find a way. I've never known a more stubborn woman."

Grinning, she smacked him in the arm. "Not as stubborn as you."

"Mayhap...mayhap," he said, and laughed. Then his handsome features turned somber as he picked up the flint and fire steel and weighed them in his hand thoughtfully.

Ásta waited for him to speak, expecting another lesson.

"You know that these are the most important tools we carry."

She nodded. He had said it so often that she was tired of hearing it.

"This steel belonged to my mother. She used it every day to keep us warm and fed. After her death, it became mine to pass along to my wife so she may keep my children warm and safe." His hand reached for hers, turning it over and then gently placing the steel in her palm. "I want you to have it."

Ásta gasped. The cold steel in her hand felt as heavy as the gesture Dànel made in gifting her this family heirloom. Could she accept?

"Nei. I cannot..." She shook her head. It was too much.

His hand slid over hers, curling her fingers over the steel. "I want you to have it, Ásta. Each day you use it to keep our child warm, you will honor my mother."

Tears gathering in her eyes, a warm glow filled Ásta. Dànel was a good, kind man.

"I will treasure it." She smiled, letting the emotion on her face show him how touched she was by the gesture.

Letting his hand fall from hers, he picked up the matching pouch. "Store it in this and fasten it to your belt."

"My thanks."

His jaw tensed when her fingers brushed over his palm as she took the pouch. A flash of unrestrained longing lit his dark eyes, before he shuttered his gaze and rose to his feet.

Her breath caught as she suddenly found herself faced with the sizable bulge in his breeches. Gods, she had forgotten what it felt like to be desired by a man. Unbidden, her breasts ached, and heat pooled between her thighs at the sight of his obvious ardor. *Goodness, was everything about this man strong, hard, and impressive?* Blushing furiously, she looked away as Dànel crossed to the bags of supplies.

"Now we can roast the duck."

CHAPTER EIGHT

ÁSTA

Tyr's hooves crunched in the snow, beating in rhythm with the birdsong that chattered overhead. It was long past dawn, yet the eerie glow of day felt especially gloomy and dark. In the short time since they'd packed up camp, the cold had become almost unbearable and the snowfall much heavier.

Ásta watched a drift of heavy snow fall from a branch onto the glistening white trail. Shivering, she leaned back against the warmth of Dànel's chest, having long given up trying to keep space between them as they rode. Nowadays, she gladly endured the sensual rhythmic sway of their hips and press of their bodies in exchange for his warmth.

"Are you well?" he asked.

"Já. It is just the cold."

Tugging the furs tighter, he wrapped his arm around her waist and pulled her back firm against him.

The brush of his hard muscles against her back made her heart flutter wildly in her chest. There was no denying it—her body ached for his touch. Ever since they'd stopped fighting something had changed between them. A bond had formed, and then deepened with each shared laugh, heated look, and lingering touch. It was a beautiful torment to crave the comfort of his warm body against hers, yet with each passing day that he didn't touch her, find no relief. Mayhap it was the baby that made her feel so? Rúna had spoken of her unquenchable need when she was with child.

"See how the snow dips over there?" Dànel said, interrupting her musings as he pointed to the left of the trail to where the trees thinned and the dazzling white of the tundra began.

Ásta scanned the frozen landscape until her eyes found the almost barely visible dip in the snowy expanse that appeared to stretch to the horizon.

"I see it." She waited for the explanation she knew was coming. She'd come to enjoy these lessons about the landscape and how his people survived the long winters on the land.

"That is a sign that the ground beneath is not solid. It may be just a hole, but this far north it is most likely much deeper."

"It is dangerous?"

"Já. Sometimes there is a large crack in the ice below, but snow has fallen to conceal it. It is a sure death if you step on it and fall in."

Ásta shivered. "That sounds terrible."

"It is a painful death. All snow is not alike—you must be wary when you walk this land."

"Who taught you this?"

Dànel paused so long that Ásta wondered if he had heard her.

"My father, before he sent me away."

She twisted to look at him. "Your father sent you away?"

A moment of discomfort crossed his face."I was fostered to Jarl Eriksson when I was but a boy."

Ásta balked at the thought of him as a young boy living amongst strangers. He must have been terrified. Was this a custom of his people?

"Will you send our child away too?" she asked, needing to know, but also dreading his answer.

A sudden anger lit Dànel's eyes. "Never," he hissed vehemently. "Our little one will know his family."

At his words, her concern melted into a teasing smile. "His? It could be a girl."

Dànel's lips twitched in the corners as she taunted him yet again. It was an argument they had repeated many times in the last few days—her sure it was a girl, and him convinced it was a boy. His dark lashes lowered, and he gazed at her through half-closed lids, his brown eyes blazing down into hers with an unrestrained hunger that made her pulse jump.

"If it is a girl, she will be as beautiful as her mother."

Ásta swallowed hard and looked away, alarmed that his searching gaze might discover reciprocated yearning in her eyes.

He pulled her back firm against him once more. "I will be a good father to our child, Ásta," he whispered in her ear. "I swear you both will be safe and have all you desire."

Her breath caught in her throat. How had she ever thought that this man would not want the burden of a child? She'd completely misjudged him.

"Ásta."

She jolted at Dànel's sharp tone, and then realized that they'd stopped moving. Was something wrong? Twisting around, she peered back at him.

"Já?"

Brow furrowed, he repeated himself. "What do you hear?"

Ásta paused, suddenly aware that the forest was quiet. No birds sang, nor was there the crunchy rustle of animals scurrying across the thick mounds of snow. Yet, there was something else...a distant roar that floated on the breeze.

"The animals are quiet but there's a hum," she said.

"Silence means danger is near. The animals have returned to

the safety of their homes and that hum is a storm heading toward us. You must never ignore silence in the forest. Now what do you smell?"

Ásta sniffed cautiously, unwilling to inhale any more than was necessary of the air that was so cold that it felt like it was freezing her on the inside.

"Hurry, Ásta. There is no time for delay, you need to know this for when I leave you at the hut."

Instantly, her chest tightened at the thought of being left alone in the forest. She'd become so accustomed to Dànel's warmth and protection that she'd forgotten he would eventually be leaving her behind. Ignoring the discomfort that thought brought, she sucked in another shaky breath.

"The air smells... moist...and damp?"

"Good. That is the scent of a snowstorm."

"A snowstorm?"

"Já. They kill quickly out here. We need to make camp, fast." Quickly dismounting, he lifted her to the ground then tugged at the ties that held the lávvu in place.

Ásta hastily collected firewood as he began erecting the tent. They carried a few days of wood supply with their food, but most days Dànel used the axe to cut fresh logs to dry by the fire to replace what they used. From his quickened pace she could tell that there would be no time for that, so she would gather what she could from nearby and dry it by the fire overnight.

As she gathered her pile and made her way back to the tent, the blustering winds blew a heavy cloud of snow in her face.

"Go inside and make the fire," Dànel shouted. "I will secure Tyr and bring the bags."

"Will Tyr be too cold outside?" She longed for a warm fire to rid the chill from her bones, but she needed to be sure that the grouchy mount she had come to adore would not be suffering in the cold.

"Nei. He shall have extra furs to keep him warm."

A short while later, Ásta stood warming her hands over a fire that was lopsided but burning strong and warming the small tent. Each day the task became a little easier, but it would be a long while before she could match Dànel's towering infernos.

"If Rúna could see me now." She smiled and shook her head. Making fires, sleeping in the forest, her friend would not recognize her. She unrolled the furs and laid them just beyond the stone circle, knowing they would need to be close to the fire for the cold night ahead.

"Ásta..." A blast of frigid air swept through the tent as Dànel stumbled inside, the bags he carried thumping as they hit floor.

Blessed Freya! What had happened to him?

She stood frozen, shocked by his ashen face and the sight of his once-dark lashes and brows coated in thick white icicles that clung to the hair like little teeth.

Shoulders shaking and teeth chattering, he swayed unsteadily for a few moments and then fell to his knees with a mighty groan.

"Nei!" Ásta rushed to his side and fell to her knees, flinching as her hand touched his ice-cold face.

"Ásta…" he mumbled.

"By the gods, you are frozen." Her heart thundered in her chest like a herd of wild horses on the run.

Then, his glazed eyes rolled into the back of his head and he collapsed, hitting the ground with a sickening thump.

Terror filled her.

Shallow breathing, pale, shivering, unconscious. Dànel had all of the signs he'd taught her of a body that was nearing death from exposure to the cold. He was not long for this world.

Think. Think. She couldn't lose him. She would not lose another man she loved. The shocking revelation crashed down over her, and then a heartbeat later panic forced her into action. She loved him. He would not die, she'd not allow it.

Grabbing him under the arms, she tugged with all her

strength, but he was as unmovable as a wall of ice, and near as cold too.

"Come on, Dànel," she urged when he groaned.

Relentlessly, she tugged and cursed him until he crawled near the fire and collapsed.

"Furs, more furs." After wrapping him in all of the furs they had, she placed more logs on the fire.

Silently entreating Freya and all the gods, Ásta knelt beside Dànel and placed a hand on his forehead.

He was still too cold. He was shivering less, but his lips remained a dangerous tinge of blue.

A string of curses fell from her lips when she slid her hands beneath the pile of furs. His chest was still cold. Why wasn't he getting warmer?

She had to heat him up, fast. Body heat! He'd told her it was the quickest way to warm someone.

Lifting the corner of the furs, she slid in, gasping as his cold tunic hit her back and moisture seeped though her dress.

"Fool!" No wonder he was not warming—he was wet. "Arms up." After removing his breeches and pulling the damp fabric of his shirt up over his head, she quickly wiped the remaining moisture from his body with a dry cloth and replaced the furs. How had he gotten wet?

Ásta pushed a rolled-up fur beneath his lolling head and put another log on the fire. A few moments later her damp dress and shift were off and she lay facing him beneath the furs.

Placing a hand on his chest, she felt the shallow jerky movements as he struggled to breathe. She shuffled closer, until her breasts moulded to his bare chest and her protruding stomach pressed against the muscular ridges of his abdomen.

Dànel released a low rumbling moan, his arms encircling her waist as his head fell into the crook of her neck.

They lay like that for a long while, Ásta brushing her fingers through his hair and begging the gods for his life as he slept. A coil of warmth crept across her chest and wrapped around the heart she'd thought long dead and buried with Njal, and latched on. She had loved her husband, yet she wanted Dànel with a ferocity far stronger than anything she'd felt with Njal.

The blustering storm had set in when Dànel finally shifted and murmured something intelligible into the crook of her neck.

Holding him tight, she remembered the night she had conceived their babe, how she had fallen apart in his arms and soared, feeling as though she could reach the gods and bend them to her will. It was not loneliness that had drawn her to Dànel, but the way he made her feel—strong and confident like the woman she used to be.

"Forgive me, Njal," she whispered, and somehow in uttering the apology aloud she found clarity. Njal would want her to have a family and find happiness. It would pain him greatly to see what she had become, a mere shadow of the woman he had wed. Loving another did not mean that she loved Njal any less, or diminish the love they had shared. She needed to begin building a life for herself and her child—with Dànel. It was time to let go of Njal and live again.

"Ásta?" Dànel nuzzled at her neck, making her shiver.

"I am here," she said, running her hands through his long dark hair. "I'm not going anywhere." The tension eased from her body as she accepted the truth behind her words. She could not lie to herself any longer—she loved Dànel.

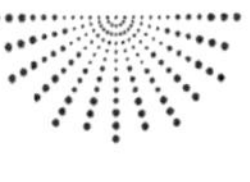

CHAPTER NINE

*D*ànel inhaled the sweet scent of pine needle soap as his hand caressed a bare back and slender hips.

Ásta. He'd know her smell anywhere.

She laid her hand against his chest. "You're warm," she said in that soft whisper he loved.

"Ásta?" he pleaded, as his fingers tightened on her firm bottom. He didn't know how it had happened and he didn't care—Ásta was naked in his arms and he wasn't letting go. Opening his eyes, Dànel pulled back and looked up at her face glowing in the firelight, her freckles sparkling like a horde of precious jewels. Gods, she was breathtaking.

"I know why I bedded you," she said softly, her lips curving tenderly in the corners as she looked down her delicate straight nose at him.

His heart raced. Something had changed in Ásta while he had slept. Gone was the deep sorrow and pain from her gaze, replaced by admiration and…a fiery longing that heated his blood.

"Why?"

"You never treated me like I was broken. Everyone in

Luleavst, even Rúna, was so afraid to upset me, like they thought I would crack open. I was so unsure of myself that when everyone saw me as broken and wounded, I believed them and became that person. But then you came, and when you looked at me I remembered who I was before Njal died, and I wanted to be that person again, even for a few moments."

All thoughts of resisting her disappeared. His hands explored the curves of her bottom with renewed vigor as he succumbed to the irresistible need to make love to her and chase away any of her lingering doubts or fears. Passion blazed within him as he surrendered to the truth in a blinding moment of pure clarity—he loved her. His hand stilled as the weight of that took root and settled within him.

"Touch me," Ásta whimpered, and her arm wrapped around his neck and pulled him closer.

Almost groaning at her needy breathless plea, his hands roamed her supple flesh, desperate to know every dip and curve of her changing body. He wanted to burn every moment of this night into his mind. Caressing her swollen belly brought on a sudden wave of possessiveness—they were his, her and the child. He flicked his tongue over the soft flesh behind her ear, sucked her earlobe into his mouth and then gave it a tender nip.

Ásta released a husky moan of approval.

"You belong in my arms," Dànel told her. "So warm..."

He cupped the underside of her soft breasts.

"So perfect." He kissed her slender neck, and then down toward her nipples, furled tight under the teasing strokes of his thumbs.

She was a feast for the eyes—her pale skin as pure as fresh snow, her freckles tempting him like sweet treats. He wanted to flick the tip of his tongue over each charming brown spot, but he knew she needed more from him right now.

"Dànel," she whimpered, and then threw her head back as he

reached his destination and took her nipple into his mouth and suckled.

His heart raced. He wanted to make her whisper his name like that over and over, he wanted her to beg, to cry out his name as she crested. It had been sweet torture lying beside her each night hoping that she would reach out and seek the comfort of his touch. She'd been so near, yet so far away, with her heart and body still devoted to her dead husband.

Dànel lifted his head and looked into her face.

Her lashes opened lazily. "What is wrong?" she asked, her eyebrows furrowing.

"It is naught." He shook his head.

Ásta quirked an eyebrow and waited, seemingly oblivious to the affect that her bared chest had on him.

"Am I dreaming?" he wondered aloud.

Smiling, she shook her head. "You were dazed and almost frozen when you stumbled inside, but you're not dreaming."

Dànel cocked his head and listened to the howling winds of the storm that continued outside. He laid his head on the folded fur pillow facing her.

"I was cold?"

Fascinated, he watched as a stray auburn tendril fell over her shoulder, covering her left breast when she nodded.

"Your eyelashes were frozen solid. I was so worried."

Hope swelled as he saw emotion that he'd never seen before in her eyes, affection and a vulnerableness that made his heart sing.

"You were?"

Sliding his leg between hers, he wrapped an arm around her and pulled her closer, until their noses almost touched.

"I was terrified."

His body heated with her admission. Then she traced her fingertips along his jaw, cupped his cheek and brushed her thumb across his bottom lip and he was instantly harder that he'd ever been in his life.

"I thought I was going to lose you," she continued.

A soft warmth filled him as he searched her gaze for answers. She'd been concerned for him? Were her feelings as deep as his own were?

"I made the fire, and still you would not get warm. I didn't realize that your tunic was wet beneath your furs. I took it off and warmed you with my body heat like you taught me."

By the gods, she was the most remarkable woman he'd ever known. He had no doubt that she'd saved his life. Without her quick actions, he'd be long dead.

"You didn't want to lose me?"

A blush crept across her cheeks. "I couldn't bear the thought." Her bottom lip quivered, but Ásta held his gaze.

Dànel lay motionless, rendered speechless by her honesty. *How does she feel about me?*

The unrestrained emotion in her eyes answered his unspoken question. *I'm afraid to let another man into my heart. I like you.*

And, the one that stole the air from his lungs.

I see you, Dànel. I see you. Her eyelids drooped to half-mast, and a raw desperation that matched his swept across her face.

"Tell me," he whispered, as he rested his head on his hand and looked down at her. He needed to hear the words from her, to know that she wanted him, that she was his. He leaned down until his lips hovered so close he could taste her breath.

"Tell me, Ásta."

Her voice hitched as she gave him what he needed. "I never want to lose you."

"That wasn't what I meant, and you know it. Say it, my sweet," he demanded.

Her tongue glided across her bottom lip, leaving behind a

glistening sheen. Then her lips parted, and her voice was silky and heavy with ardent intent. "I want you."

Hel! He had to taste her, now. Dànel crushed his mouth to hers, his tongue darting out to savor her sweetness. When her tongue met his and she moaned softly into his mouth, he was sure he had died and gone to Valhalla. Thor's hammer! He kissed her as if he was a starved man and she was his succulent salvation.

Ásta moved her hips, rocking her sex against his thigh.

His cock jumped as he slid his hand between her legs. Sliding his fingers upward, he found the bundle of nerves that would send her soaring.

Ásta froze mid-kiss, her breath catching with a delightful gasp.

Dànel tore his mouth from hers. "Breathe, my sweet," he whispered, stroking her hair back from her face.

Sucking in a shaky breath, she rocked against his hand, sending the tips of his fingers flicking across her tender nub.

Dànel swallowed a groan and pressed harder, giving her the friction she needed.

Her hands found his shoulders, gripping tightly for advantage as she rocked back and forth on his fingers.

She was stunning. More beautiful even, than the nine wave maidens who had led many a Viking warrior to a watery grave.

"Já," Ásta whispered, and threw her head back as he slid two fingers inside her and drove her nearer to the edge.

"Come apart for me, my sweet."

Her back arched, and her fingers clenched around handfuls of the soft fur bed.

Dànel burned the memory of her like this into his mind.

"Next time I will slide inside you and make you mine," he promised as he thrust deeper, almost exploding himself when he latched on to one of her dusky swollen nipples and felt her tighten around his fingers.

A keening cry fell from her lips as she shuddered in his arms, before sagging back into the furs, eyes closed and replete.

Óðinn be damned. The goddess, Hel, could take him now. He would go to his death willingly now that he'd seen her like this—eyes closed, chest heaving, and a sated smile on her face. He was rock hard and aching to make love to her, but the rest of him wouldn't cooperate. His body needed rest and time to recover.

Dànel watched as the heated flush of her skin receded and her breathing eased into the soft lull of sleep. Ásta belonged with him. He knew it now and he'd know it until the last breath left his body. He added a log to the smouldering fire, pulled the furs tight around them, and closed his eyes.

Ásta snuggled backward until her bottom pressed against his leg.

Dànel curved his body around hers and let the heavy pull of sleep take him. For now, he would hold her in his arms, but tomorrow he'd make her his woman.

CHAPTER TEN

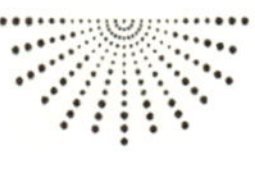

ÁSTA

Ásta hobbled toward the sod hut perched between last of the thinning forest and the vast empty tundra.

"It looks old," she said, holding back a disappointed sigh.

"It will be warmer than in the tent," Dànel said, as he dumped the bags inside, sending up a cloud of dust.

Her face flushed at the reminder of what had happened in the tent last eve. She'd been relieved when they had woken to find the storm had blown over and Dànel had hurried to break camp and get back on the trail. She had spent the day riding Tyr alone, whilst Dànel led them safely through the towering snow-drifts left behind by the storm, until they'd finally reached this hut on the edge of the bleak tundra that felt like the edge of the world.

"I swear I'd do anything to see the sun again," Ásta muttered, turning her face upward wistfully. She loathed the eerie glow that the long dark winter days cast upon this land.

"Spring will be here before long."

Ásta glanced at the small sod hut nestled against the pine trees, and then back at the flat landscape with shards of ice rolling across the deep fresh snow. Hopefully the hut would at least keep out the howling wind.

"Can you unpack? And I will chop some firewood while there is still light."

"Já. It looks like it needs cleaning," she agreed.

Dànel returned to his weary stallion and patted him affectionately on the nose. "Tyr will be glad for a decent rest."

"He deserves it," she agreed wholeheartedly, knowing they would not have made it to the safety of this place without the feisty stallion. Pressing a hand to her aching back, she watched Dànel lead Tyr toward the animal shelter, the swagger of the man perfectly matched to that of his powerful mount. How was he so nonchalant when she felt like she'd awakened from a deep slumber to find the world bathed in light? Everything was brighter, and she was aware of Dànel like never before. When would he touch her again?

As though sensing her gaze, Dànel turned and looked over his shoulder, tossing her a knowing smile before he disappeared behind the log building.

A delicious throb pulsed between her legs. She had a feeling he wouldn't hold back next time. Forcing the distracting thoughts from her mind, she approached the lopsided hut and looked at it more closely.

On closer inspection the small round-like structure seemed stable enough, and the rough-cut birch logs covered in thick sod looked like they would keep the cold winds out. A few spindly saplings grew on the roof, but the walls appeared solid, and the door was still latched tight when they'd arrived so at least she wouldn't have to deal with unwanted critters.

She quickly busied herself with making the space comfortable to sleep and eat in. With a birchwood broom she swept the layer of dust from the floors, then spread the tanned hides over the floor, coaxed a fire to life in the central fire pit, and laid the furs out near the warmth.

"It is small, but it will be enough while Dànel is gone."

She hated that Dànel was going to leave her to go find Mattias. She'd never been alone, ever. All she'd ever known was the busy courts of her father and Njal, and then she'd been with Rúna. The thought of endless silence and facing the dangers of this harsh landscape alone was terrifying. There would be nobody to care for her or keep her safe. She would have to do it for herself. Was she strong enough to do that? Or would she die out here all alone, like a weakened animal unable to survive the harsh conditions?

Shaking off the gloomy thoughts, she walked back outside in search of Dànel. Following the sounds of his axe hitting wood, she walked around the back of the animal shelter and...

Stopped in her tracks. *Bestla, mother of Óðinn!*

Dànel stood bare-chested with his long dark hair flowing down his back, his powerful arms thrusting the axe above his head and then striking downward with an easy grace. Sweat ran down the hard planes of his wide chest, racing toward his rippling stomach and reindeer-skin breeches.

Her nipples hardened at the unexpected vision.

He looked like a god, a dark god against a white backdrop conquering the freshly felled tree. In the muted light it seemed as though the snow-laden trees behind Dànel recognized him as a part of the earth that gave them life and held him in their embrace.

Ásta's heart swelled at the sight. Slowly, along their journey, Dànel had reclaimed that connection to the north that had seemed so lost to him when she'd arrived. In showing her how to survive, he had found where he belonged.

His head snapped up, as though he sensed her hungry gaze.

"Is all well?" He leaned on the handle of his axe and wiped the sweat from his face with the back of his hand.

"Já," she stuttered. *How was he not cold?*

He arched a brow at her.

She shuffled backward, too caught up in imagining the taste of the salty shimmering droplet sliding over his left nipple to hide her thoughts from showing on her face.

His hand tightened on the axe handle the moment he recognized her desire.

Ásta shuddered as he stepped toward her, his gaze darkening with sinful intent. A flood of pleasure heated between her legs.

"I…I am…" Lost for words, she spun around and marched back the cabin, her ears burning and his triumphant laughter ringing in her ears.

"More tempting than cool mead on a midsummer's day," she muttered as she paused to scoop snow into the two wooden pails outside the door. With just a look Dànel set her body so ablaze that her touch could have melted all of the ice giants in Jotunheimr. Not even an ice bath would extinguish the fire he lit within her.

~

"Gods, woman." Dànel's voice was a hoarse rumble behind her.

Ásta froze with the damp cloth in her hand. She'd thought she would have longer to complete her bathing before he finished chopping the felled tree. Wrapping her arms over her chest and ignoring the water dripping down her forearm, she turned to look over her shoulder and braced herself for his reaction. He'd never hidden his desire for her and now she was naked in front of him.

Dànel looked at her as if he were ravenous, his rugged handsome face moving up and down as his dark eyes roaming her exposed flesh.

The taut veins in his neck bulged as he swallowed hard and then groaned her name "Ásta."

She could almost taste his lust in the air between them as his eyes swept down her back to where her hair hung loose, the tips teasing the swell of her bare ass.

His nostrils flared and her heart skipped at the wildness in his eyes. Striding toward her, his muscles moving with the same tense exactness as a lynx preparing to pounce, he looked every bit like a man with the heart of a Viking warrior.

"Let me," he said, reaching for the damp cloth.

She turned and looked down at the steaming bowl of water on the rough timber counter, her chest tightening into a hard knot as she clenched the cloth, unwilling to relinquish the damp fabric to his strong fingers. Could she let him bathe her as her Njal once had?

"I'm not..." she stammered, before her voice trailed off.

Dànel pressed his bare chest against her back.

Her eyes drifted closed, making her instantly more aware of the heat where their bodies touched and how unbelievably right it felt. She was his, with every breath in her body, she was his. She delighted in his musky masculine scent and the evidence of his desire that pressed hard against her buttocks. When had he removed his pants?

His hand slid up her neck, cupped her chin, and turned her head toward him. "Look at me," he demanded, his voice a low seductive growl that made her spirit soar.

Ásta forced herself to meet his steady gaze, her breath catching at the raw passion she saw reflected back at her. Her heart lurched, and then danced like the call of the hunting drum.

His roughened fingertips tucked a strand of stray hair behind her ear, and when he brushed his thumb across her bottom lip a calm settled over her. This was different, so very different from what she'd felt with Njal, as different as a soft breeze and a blustering gale.

"Let go, Ásta."

Unclenching her fingers, she released the damp cloth. It

fell into his waiting hand, taking with it the last of her resistance. She would carry the memories of Njal with her forever, but it was time to move on with this man who held her so tenderly.

"You will never regret giving me your trust." The tension eased from his body as he made the somber promise and his hand tightened around the damp fabric. He spun her around in his embrace and groaned as her breasts pressed against his chest.

"You make me burn, my sweet."

Ásta laid her cheek in the warm pocket where his chest met his neck, and inhaled the sweet tangy scent of him. Blessed Freya, he smelt earthy and delicious.

"I want you too," she whispered.

Water sloshed in the bowl on the counter behind her.

The hair on her neck rose, accompanied by a delightful shiver as Dànel pressed the warm cloth to her back and ran it down her spine.

She wrapped an arm around his neck, needing to hold on lest her knees give out. And when the soft caress of the cloth disappeared, she missed his touch as the sun missed the moon.

He dropped to his knees and gently wiped the swell of her stomach.

"Our baby," he whispered reverently.

She looked down at him through heavy lids, her heart filled with joy at the thought of raising their child together.

"Our *first* baby."

His eyes shot up to hers, his throat bobbing as he gulped.

They stayed like that for a long moment, the weight of her words and the commitment they heralded stretching like an invisible bond between them.

"Our first," he repeated.

Smiling wryly, he skimmed the cloth over her breasts and circled her swollen nipples.

"Gods, I want you. You look like Freya with your soft curves and your breasts heavy and ready to nurture our child."

Ásta whimpered at hearing how he desired her just as much like this as when her body had been firm and lean. He left her breathless when his hand slid between her legs, rubbing the cloth back and forth over her bare sex much longer than was necessary. She needed a few moments to regain control.

"Now me," she demanded, taking the cloth and bowl from him and walking to the fire. It was her turn to make him ache. Bending over, she tipped the dirty water into the empty pail and refilled the bowl.

"Gods' blood! Get back over here, woman."

Ásta smiled at his reaction to the sight of her bent over at the waist. He could see everything, just as she'd intended.

"Just a moment." Straightening with the steaming bowl in her hands, Ásta turned and boldly swayed her hips as she walked back to him. She was desperate to feel him inside her, but first she would care for him as he had her.

When she placed the bowl on the counter, he pulled her into his arms. She knew that look—he was moments away from losing control. His head dipped, his hungry gaze fixated on her lips.

"Not yet," she scolded, and pushed him away. "My turn."

"I need..."

A shudder wracked his body as she trailed the warm cloth down over his chest, squeezing his nipple between her finger and thumb and then forging a damp path down to his waist.

"You need to wait."

On the way back up, she avoided his thick rod standing upright against his stomach. She shuddered as she fought back the urge to drop to her knees and worship him with her mouth.

"So strong," she said, as she turned her attention to his muscular arms, watching the glistening droplets run down the hard muscle. "I have never felt safer than last night, wrapped in your arms as I drifted off to sleep."

Clenching his hands into fists at his sides, a slow hiss escaped Dànel as she knelt and washed his muscular legs from the ankle to the groin.

"Gods, Ásta. Please don't stop now."

A laugh escaping her chest, she rose to her feet and leaned in until her lips hovered tantalizingly close to his. "*Nothing* would make me stop now."

The air crackled between them, as dangerous and seductive as stolen moments with a forbidden lover.

Heart racing, Ásta wrapped the cloth around his rigid member and reveled in the dazed look in his eyes when she slid her hand up and down.

His eyes drifted closed and he threw his head back.

She loved holding him like this and controlling his pleasure. Tossing the cloth aside, she took him in her hand and increased the pace, her breath quickening as she lost herself in the carnal thrusting of his hips and the powerful feeling of his silky manhood sliding through her hand.

Dànel froze mid-thrust, his eyes snapping open. "Now, woman," he growled, brooking no argument as he picked her up, crossed the room in two strides, and lowered her into the fur bedding.

Wrapping her arms around his neck, she pulled him down with her, a surge of heat tearing through her when his thick cock settled between her legs.

"I need you." His masculine growl made her sex ache.

"I need you too."

DÁNEL

*D*ànel licked at the freckle that taunted him from the crevasse at the corner of Ásta's glistening lips. Óðinn, he was painfully hard. He crushed his mouth to hers, his senses reeling as Ásta kissed him back, her slow exploration like a soothing balm to his racing heart.

He wanted to taste her. All of her.

Trailing a path of kisses down her chest, he slowly licked one of her pebbled nipples then took it into his mouth.

"Oh," she gasped, as he suckled on the furled bud and then teased it with quick flicks of his tongue. When her hips bucked upward and her wet warmth pressed into his hard flesh, his tenuous restraint snapped. He couldn't wait a moment longer. He lifted his head, needing to see the look on her face as they joined.

"Dànel," she panted, as he aligned his cock with her welcoming heat. Her arm slid up and around his neck, and then she stretched up to brush her lips across his.

"Mine," she whispered.

Dànel shuddered as she laid claim to him, his already hammering heart jumping to his throat. Then, as her tight heat wrapped around him and she looked up at him lovingly, he vowed he would forgo Valhalla if he could die in her arms.

"I don't want to hurt the baby."

She brushed the hair from his face and smiled. "You won't."

Relieved, he moved faster, careful to keep his weight off her stomach.

"Oh." This time her sigh was breathy and thick with satisfaction. Her hands gripped his hair and pulled his head down, her mouth devouring his as he lost all control and thrust hard, cupping her full breasts in his hands and plucking at her hard nipples.

"Harder," she begged, wrapping her long legs around his waist and matching his primal rhythm.

Rising above her, he plunged deep and fast into the divine vision below him.

She was so damn beautiful as she neared release with her eyes closed, head thrown back and her auburn hair glowing like a beacon against the dark furs.

Sliding his hand down the center of her chest to the soft hair between her legs, he rubbed his thumb across her swollen nub. He almost exploded when her mouth fell open in surprise as he tenderly pinched the source of her pleasure. This woman owned him.

"Dànel," she moaned, throwing her hands above her head and thrusting her swollen breasts up.

He rose up onto his knees, gripped her hips, and thrust harder, determined to give her what she needed.

Suddenly, her lips parted in a silent cry.

Involuntary tremors wracked his body. She was so damned beautiful as she chased her release. Ásta was his. Finally, she was his woman.

A heartbeat later, she tightened around him, her body milking him as she shuddered and then soared.

"Mine," Dànel roared, thrusting one last time and giving her his seed. He'd never get enough of her, never.

As her breathing slowed, her hands feathered down his back. "That was..."

"That was everything," he agreed, lowering himself down beside where she'd melted into the furs. "You are incredible."

She rolled toward him, her mouth curving into a shy smile when he pulled a fur over them both.

"Sleep now, my love," he said, pulling her close and smiling when her eyes closed lazily and she snuggled into his chest. There was something so right about watching his woman sleep and memorizing each freckle on her slender nose, her kissable lips, and the auburn locks spread out behind her in a tangled mess. Ásta was his world now, her and the life that they had created together. He knew that he was on the right path once more, that holding Ásta like this in his arms was exactly where he was supposed to be.

Come dawn, he would hunt and eliminate the threat to his family.

CHAPTER ELEVEN

*Á*sta's stomach dropped as she watched Dànel secure the last pack to his saddle beside his hunting bow. A wave of apprehension swept over her. She didn't want him to go. The thought of being alone here in the wilderness knowing that Mattias was coming for her, made bile rise to the back of her throat. Choking it back down, she bit her bottom lip. Even though she knew Dànel needed to go back to stop Mattias, her whole being screamed at her to beg him to stay.

After fastening the last buckle, Dànel turned to her, his expression serious. She could tell that his mind was already focused on the grim task ahead, but his gaze softened when he saw the worry on her face.

"You are just one man against many." Her voice shook as the panic crept in. She couldn't lose him, not now that she had fallen in love with him. She wouldn't survive losing another man she loved at Mattias' hand. It would break her completely.

"You forget that the battlefield is mine. They will never outmatch me on this land," Dànel said with such confidence that she almost believed him.

"You are safe. I will stop Mattias long before he reaches here."

Ásta rested a hand on her stomach, unable to shake the terrible foreboding that was making her gut churn.

"And if you can't?"

Tyr snorted and shuffled impatiently.

Dànel pulled her into his arms. "That won't happen, my love," he said, and kissed the top of her head.

She buried her face against his neck, his earthy scent failing to subdue her panic as she voiced her worst fears. "Mattias always gets what he wants."

"Not this time."

The emotion she'd been holding back escaped and tears rolled down her cheeks. She wanted to believe Dànel, but she couldn't fathom being free of the darkness and fear that had haunted her for years.

"Look at me, Ásta." Dànel put his hand under her chin and tipped her head back, his thumb brushing away her tears.

She gazed at him through the moisture brimming in her lower lids.

"You are strong, and you are brave. I know that you can take care of yourself out here. I would never leave you if I thought otherwise."

Ásta fought back the second flood of tears and nodded. If he believed she could do it, then she would too. She needed to be strong for him and their baby.

"Mattias will never hurt you again," he promised, then lowered his mouth to hers and coaxed her into a slow lingering kiss that made her head spin.

She suppressed a whimper when he finally pulled away. "I shall make an offering to the gods each day until you return to me," she vowed.

"Such favor is sure to hasten my journey." He kissed her

softly one last time, and then backed away from her and swung up into the saddle.

"Remember to keep the wood dry and don't stray far from the hut."

"Don't worry about us. We shall be here, waiting for you." Ásta smiled bravely, though the cold hard lump in her gut made her want to heave as Daniel rode onto the trail that led toward the mountain ridge. She stood watching until he disappeared into the frozen forest, then her chest tightened until it was hard to breathe. She was alone.

Crack.

As a branch snapped and fell to the earth with a heavy thud, Ásta picked up her skirts and fled back to the safety of the hut. Her whole body shook as she slammed the door and collapsed against it with tears rolling down her cheeks.

Dànel should never have left her out here alone.

She couldn't do this.

~

The wind ripped the door from Ásta's hand, slamming it open so hard she thought it would surely break. Before stepping outside she paused to check that her cloak was buttoned, and her fur was tightly secured by the silver pin.

Latching the door, she made her way over the well-trodden trail to the outhouse. In the days since Dànel had left, she had settled into being alone and found herself falling in with the natural rhythms of the land—rising to traipse through the dawn fog to relieve herself, spending the warmest part of the day outside doing chores, and then retiring early. It felt good to know she could survive here alone. Dànel would be proud. Yesterday she'd even stayed outside until dark to watch the snow geese rise up into the smoky darkness and fly away from the blackening clouds rolling across the sky. The blustering storm hadn't bothered her—she'd just sat by the fire sewing a blanket for the baby and listening to the creaking trees and howling wind.

She had felt the first fluttering of life in her belly this morn, and her heart had filled with joy at the thought of sharing that with Dànel when he returned. Constantly worrying about Dànel was exhausting, but now she could comfort herself with thoughts of placing his hand on her stomach to feel their baby's first kicks.

Gathering her fur cloak carefully, she squatted over the outhouse pit and released her aching bladder. Oh, the relief! Then, just as she completed her other needs, she heard a hollow crunch in the forest to her left. *What was that?* Her head snapped up. Rising to her feet, she pulled the blade from her pocket, her eyes searching the tree line.

An icy shiver crept up her spine.

She'd become used to the noises of the animals here, the soft thumps of the hares scampering about and the pitter-patter of the stealthy foxes that hunted them, but that had sounded bigger, heavier. Mayhap as heavy as a man?

Knowing there was no time for hesitation, she dashed back along the trail with her heart hammering in her chest.

Something was wrong. She could feel it in her bones.

Yanking the door closed behind her, she a slid the wooden barricade in place and fell back against it panting. The blade shook in her trembling hand. She placed it in her lap and inhaled shaky breaths until the tightness in her chest eased.

"A moose. It could have been a moose," she told herself.

There were many things that could have made the noise other than the man she abhorred—a stray moose that hadn't moved south with the herd, or a bear sniffing around at the new smells in its territory.

Ásta looked around the cosy hut and sighed in relief. She couldn't be sure, so she would stay inside just to be safe. She had everything she needed in here, and Dànel shouldn't be more than another day or two at most.

"Just stay inside and wait. You can do that." Rising to her feet, she walked to the counter intent on distracting herself by chopping the root vegetables to add to yesterday's pottage.

Nei! She stumbled back and clutched her throat, fighting for air.

The dagger she'd left on the counter stood upright, fresh blood dripping down the carved bone handle and onto the tiny severed heart pinned to the counter.

Her legs gave out and she fell to her knees, a cold sweat breaking out on her skin. One hand pressed to her chest, she gasped for air and crawled to the corner farthest from the door.

Mattias had found her.

CHAPTER TWELVE

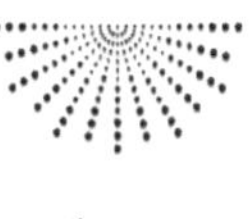

DÁNEL

ànel hid high in the branches of a large pine tree watching the slumbering encampment below.

Thinking they had the advantage being the hunter rather than the prey, the fools hadn't even tried to hide their tracks through the forest and most of the warriors had drunk ale long into the night before stumbling off to their tents. Now just three remained out in the cold, standing in a huddled group around the fire when they should have been standing guard.

"You think the king will share her around when he's done with her?" the tallest one asked his companions.

Letting his mouth form a mirthless smile, Dànel narrowed his gaze on his target. Nobody talked about his woman like that. It was time to strike and he knew who he would kill first. Pulling his bow from his back, he curled his lips back, baring his teeth as he notched an arrow and pulled the string taut. He was going to destroy every single last one of the dishonorable bastards who hunted a defenceless pregnant woman. The first arrow loosed with a satisfying twang.

The largest Viking toppled to the ground with a heavy thud, his final breath escaping his lungs with a heavy hiss.

After that Dànel found his flow, his hands moving on instinct as he released a rush of arrows in quick succession before leaping to the ground.

A second man fell to his knees, his hands clutching at the arrow through his gut attempting to staunch the flow of blood.

"Attack," the last warrior roared, snapping off the arrow impaled in his thigh while clutching his sword and eyeing Dànel warily.

Gripping his own blade, Dànel lunged, striking at the man. He needed to deal with him before the others roused. The force of their blades meeting made his arm shake, but Dànel struck out with his other hand and plunged his dagger into the man's neck.

A rush of warm blood hit Dànel in the face. He watched as the light dimmed in the warrior's eyes, and then tossed him aside to focus on the half-dressed men stumbling from their tents.

Dànel shifted from foot to foot, his body humming with the familiar vigor of battle as he roared and dispatched the enemy with the fury of an enraged bear. All sense of time and place was lost to him as he coated cold earth in a layer of thick red blood like an offering to the gods.

"You cannot win. King Mattias will have her."

Mattias! The one he had come to kill. Dànel froze mid-strike as his vengeful fog lifted.

"He knew you'd come, so we left a trail for you to find," taunted the kneeling warrior.

Dànel gazed at the bodies strewn around the camp and then down at wounded Viking. What had he said? *Mattias will have her.*

"Where is he?" Dànel hissed, his focus once again on the man he had come to kill.

"The king continued alone, so you could not track him."

Dànel's gut knotted as panic took hold. The one he hunted wasn't here.

"When did he leave?" he roared.

"You'll never reach her in time," the Viking said, an evil grin splitting his face.

Not again! Once more, he heard the loud crack as the ice gave way and watched Tóra disappear into the frigid water. *Nei!* He had walked straight into Matthias' trap. He'd left Ásta alone and unprotected against a madman.

A raw primitive grief overtook him, and he plummeted headlong into despair.

"Nei!" The strangled cry tore from his chest as he thrust his sword down using his weight to crack through ribs and pierce the scoundrel's heart.

Running back to the grove when he'd left his stallion, he threw himself up into the saddle.

Tyr reared and then leapt forward, attuned to the urgency of his master.

As they reached a gallop, Dànel leaned forward and ran his hands along his stallion's neck.

"Go, boy. Go," he urged. "Ásta needs us!"

He had to get there before Mattias. This time he would protect what was his. He couldn't lose Ásta, he wouldn't.

CHAPTER THIRTEEN

ÁSTA

Ásta sat wide-awake with the knife clutched in her trembling hand. All night she had waited for Mattias to come for her. She knew it was him, she'd heard about the sickening games he played with his women. It was said that not even his prized hounds were safe from the sting of his blades when he was in a mood. She had always known that there was something indubitably broken in his mind.

"Ásta."

Her head snapped up at the singsong taunt that broke the early morning stillness, her knuckles turning white around the bone-handled blade. He was here for her.

"Open the door and greet your husband."

Cringing, she backed away as he scraped his blade across the wooden planks that separated them.

"Open it, woman," he shouted, and then his fist pounded on the door.

Ásta whimpered and stumbled back further, pulling her furs tighter to ward off the icy chill creeping up her spine. She had one foot in the underworld, and Hel, the goddess of death, had sent Mattias to dispatch her there.

"You'll soon learn to obey," he said, when she did not respond. "Or I'll beat it into you."

When his footsteps faded away, she knew he'd be back. The door wouldn't keep him from getting what he wanted. Nothing would.

Her heartbeat thundered in her ears and her skin dampened with a terrified sweat. She needed to get out of here, away from him. Eyes darting around the hut, she searched for an escape that didn't exist. She was trapped.

Crack. The door splintered under the heavy strike of an axe.

Her heart seemed to rise up in her throat, its terrified beating pushing it out of her body as Mattias tore away her last barrier of protection in three strikes.

A gust of cold air as icy as the heart in his chest followed him inside. His hulking figure filled the room, a mountain of dark cruel intent towering above her.

Ásta felt the blood drain from her face when he brushed his dark hair from his face. She'd forgotten how much he looked like Njal with that same strong jaw and prominent nose. Mattias was an attractive man, and if not for his cruel games, he'd have had his pick of beautiful women.

Spotting her cowering in the corner, he held up his hands in a peaceful gesture and smiled at her tenderly.

"Ásta, how I have missed you, my love."

Her breath skipped as her frightened gaze catalogued every nuance of his expression. It was his eyes that gave him away, the soulless lack of humanity that rendered her just a thing, a possession, to be used and discarded. She whimpered, and her mouth filled with the foulness brought up by her churning gut.

He smiled and she thought all the muscles in her body would shatter. He was feeding on her fear. He laughed then, that same laugh that had echoed down from the ridge where he sat astride his horse watching his men kill Njal.

A sudden spark of anger flared to life within her and she

rose to her feet. He had killed her love and her baby. He was the cause of her years of darkness and despair.

"No words of love for your husband?"

Her anger became a scalding fury and she silently vowed she would rather die than spend one night in his bed. She lunged, raising the blade and aiming for his jugular.

His hand wrapped around her wrist and squeezed until the blade fell to the floor with a dull thud.

"You think you can kill me?" Mattias taunted, tossing her aside as if he was merely swatting a fly.

Ásta fell heavily, her hands shielding her belly as she bounced off the side of the hut. She pushed herself to her hands and knees, ignoring the pain in her shoulder where she'd hit the wall. Slowly, she rose to her feet and eyed Mattias warily. Would he kill her now?

Dropping his coat to the floor, he warmed his hands over the fire, acting as though it was common to seek comfort at the hearth of the woman he planned to kill.

"What do you want?" she asked.

He turned his hands to warm the back of them. "What I've always wanted—you as my wife and queen."

"I...I can't go back," she stuttered.

"You *will* be my wife, Ásta."

Dread hit her in the chest like an arrow. It was as she'd suspected—Mattias didn't just want her to warm his bed, he also needed her to keep the throne.

"You will open your thighs, or I'll wage war on your family. How well do you think your aging father would fare against me on the battlefield?"

"Please Mattias. Don't do this. I was wed to your brother. I cannot do it."

His voice lowered to a deadly hiss. "You *will* return to Jottland. And on our wedding night, I'll take you in every hole and lick your sweet blood from your skin."

Ásta whimpered at his sickening promise. By the gods, he was rotten to the core. Had he lost all reason? Was that why he'd killed his own brother? She needed to know.

"Why did you kill Njal?"

Mattias shrugged nonchalantly. "He took what was mine—the throne, you. I saw you first. You were mine long before you were his."

"You murdered him, so you could have me?" Her stomach heaved as he confirmed her horrifying suspicion that she was part of the reason Njal was dead. She took a step back at the relentless insanity in his gaze.

"You're mine and I'll never let you go. There's nowhere that I wouldn't find you, Ásta."

A cold empty numbness took hold within Ásta. She brushed away the tears that had fallen without her even realizing. It was for the best that Dànel was not here, for she couldn't bear for him to be hurt and there was no beating Mattias.

"I shall go with you," she said.

"Good. Now make me food. I've had naught but dried meat for days."

Ásta moved to the counter, her mind clouded by a thick fog as she placed her shaking hands on the flat surface.

As she reached for the dried fish, the metallic glint of the fire steel caught her eye. She slid her fingers across the cool metal, and then picked it up in the palm of her hand.

"What do you make, wife?"

"Fish stew," she replied absently as the haze faded and awareness took over. What was she doing? She couldn't cede defeat, ever. Dànel had bestowed this precious heirloom upon her the day she'd realized that. She had to get away from Mattias. A king couldn't marry a woman heavy with another man's babe, and as soon as he saw her stomach, he'd know. Thank the gods that her condition was hidden beneath her fur coat.

There are no kings and queens out here, Ásta. We all are equal on this land. It is our skills that help us to conquer and survive.

Dànel's words cut through the fog in her head and she recognized their truth. Out here Mattias was merely a man, and she just a woman. For once she held the advantage, because she understood the dangers of this wild, majestic land. It was time to fight back. She couldn't wait and hope that Dànel would come and save her. She would have to protect her baby herself. Her elbow bumped the wooden pail sitting on the counter, sloshing some water over the rim.

A man can freeze in minutes if his clothes get wet in this cold.

"Hurry up, woman."

"It's coming." Ásta fussed with the salted fish, breaking it into small pieces and tossing it into the empty pot, then risked a glance over her shoulder.

Mattias laid beside the fire, his long limbs stretched out and his eyes closed, so great was his confidence that she was under his control.

Gripping the pail in her hands, Ásta clenched her jaw and spun around. Should she do it? If he caught her, he would kill her. Either way she was dead—she would not go down without a fight. Leaping forward, she tossed the water over him, dropped the pail, and ran for the door.

Mattias roared and jumped to his feet behind her, but she was out the door before he'd begun to move.

Heart pounding in her ears, Ásta ran through the morning fog toward the barren tundra. Sinking into the soft snow up to her knees, the sharp pain in her chest screamed at her for more air as she fled the thundering footsteps of the beast chasing her.

"Stop, Ásta!" Mattias yelled. He was gaining, letting her do the hard work of cutting the path through the thick snow while he closed the gap between them.

Freya help her. Why wasn't he slowing down? He must be

beginning to freeze by now. When it was this cold, water turned to ice faster than you could drink it outside.

"Ásta..."

That sounded more like a groan than a demand.

"Shhome back..."

Her pulse jumped. He was slurring his words—the cold was starting to affect him. Soon he would be as disorientated as Dànel had been after the blizzard. She risked a look over her shoulder.

Mattias had fallen to his knees and icicles were forming on his lashes and brows that matched his ashen pallor. He glared up at her as he struggled to regain his footing, his whole body shaking from exposure to the harsh cold winds that bent this barren land to their will.

Ásta surged forward with renewed vigor. She could do this. She had a plan. This was it, her chance to save her baby. She veered left around the dip in the snow, and then back right.

"ÁSTA!" Mattias roared, his voice cracking under the strain.

She skidded to a stop and turned to face him. She would not run from him anymore.

"I'm not going with you. I am staying with Dànel. I carry his child," she said, pulling back her furs to show him her protruding stomach for a few moments before she clasped them closed again. She shoved her hands beneath the thick fur since she had no gloves and her fingers already had the prickling burn that preceded frostbite.

Struggling to hold his sword in his shaking hand, Mattias stumbled toward her. A muscle bulged in his neck as he bellowed in that deep guttural tone that haunted her in her dreams.

"Foolishh girl. Now you will die."

Ásta backed away, abandoning any hope that her words would reach through his madness and make him see reason. He was beyond help. Not even the most apt healer could cure the darkness within him.

"Don't do this," she said.

Still he advanced, the look on his face leaving no doubt of his murderous intent.

Inhaling a fortifying breath, she stood her ground. Not wanting to be responsible for taking a life, she had led Mattias to a place where his own actions would decide to his fate. She would stay until the end, her loyalty to Njal forbidding her from abandoning his brother.

Mattias stumbled when his boot disappeared below the snow and didn't find purchase.

Refusing to look away, she watched as he teetered on the edge, though she knew it may break her to watch the demise of a man that looked so much like her Njal. Despite his many crimes, she knew that Njal would not want his brother to die a lonely death. And so, she stayed, until with a harsh final roar that cut through the blustering wind, Mattias toppled forward and disappeared into the chasm below.

Exhausted, Ásta fell to her knees. She was free of him at last. It was over, finally over.

CHAPTER FOURTEEN

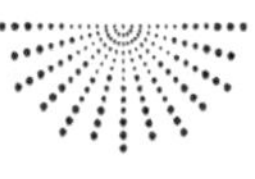

DÁNEL

Bending low over Tyr's neck, Dànel welcomed pain of branches whipping across his face that kept him alert. They were close. He had to get there in time to save her, to protect her.

The spruce forest thinned, and the little sod hut came into view.

Was the door wide open?

He squinted in the dim early morning light. *Nei!* His stomach dropped.

The pale Birchwood door was destroyed, reduced to just a few piles of splintered wood strewn across the frozen ground.

He was too late. His eyes, long dried out by the cold, began to water as he scanned the tundra. Had he missed them on the trail in his rush to get here?

A flash of red caught his eye and his heart lurched.

Ásta was running towards the open tundra, her legs struggling to push though the heavy snow drifts. Her auburn hair whipped around her face as she glanced over her shoulder at the figure chasing her.

Dànel kicked his weary mount, but Tyr could move no faster. He was spent.

Mattias was gaining on her, his arms and legs pumping furiously in his tunic and breeches.

Dànel's throat closed over—he was too far away. He would never reach Ásta in time. He watched in horror as she fell to her hands and knees in the deep snow.

"Nei!" His hands clenched so tight the leather reins cut into his palms. "Get up!" he screamed, though he knew Ásta wouldn't hear him over the wind.

She stumbled to her feet.

"Run, oh, Gods, run." He could hardly bear to watch, his breath rattling through his clenched teeth. His heart leapt to his throat when Mattias closed the gap between them. He wanted to close his eyes so he didn't have to watch another woman he loved die, but he would not abandon her, ever.

Ásta surged forward when Mattias stumbled and fell to his knees, swerving right then left, before she skidded to a halt.

Icy fear gripped his heart and began to squeeze. Why had she stopped? What was she doing? Then he saw it, the slight dip in the snow that separated her from the King. He jerked backward in shock—Ásta had lured Mattias into a trap and was using the land to protect herself. Breath flowed into his lungs a little easier. Even though he couldn't defend her, she was using what he'd taught her to save herself. He hadn't failed her after all.

Ásta's pulled her furs aside, showing the King the child in her womb.

Dànel's brow furrowed. What in Óðinn's name is she doing? Why would she deliberately goad him? She was not safe yet and there was no telling what the man would do.

The king's face contorted with rage and he rushed forward.

By the gods, she looked like a flame haired warrior, standing there conquering her fear and facing down the man that had killed her husband.

Ásta remained motionless, her jaw hard and features determined as she watched her husband's murderer topple forward and disappear into the crevasse hidden beneath the snow.

She had done it. His woman, pregnant and weapon-less, had fought back and saved herself. She had the heart of a true warrior. He manoeuvred Tyr around the deadly chasm, leapt to the ground and hurried to where she had fallen to her knees, worry for her condition erasing his thoughts of her victory.

"Ásta?"

She jerked away from his touch.

"Ásta, I'm here, my sweet," he said, coaxing her to look at him. Then he lifted her into his arms, vowing to protect her and their child until Óðinn called him to Valhalla. Now that King Mattias was dead, there was nothing that could stop him.

"Dànel?" Ásta finally whispered, her voice was shaky and weak.

"Rest, my sweet. It's over. I've got you," he promised, and strode towards the hut determined to love his warrior queen, long into the night.

CHAPTER FIFTEEN

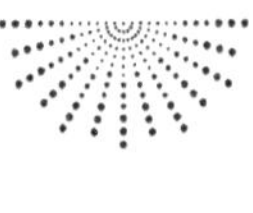

DÁNEL

Two long dark winters later, Dànel stood outside his hut watching Ásta play with their son in what was likely the last snow of the season.

Johá was born just a few months after they returned to the siida and married, his tiny body healthy and strong long before the leaves changed color the following autumn.

The sight of Ásta lifting Johá onto the little sled she'd bought at the last winter market made his heart sing as though it were humming in tune with the song of the land. They had built a good life here—he'd added three ships to Ándde's fleet and tension with the elders had vanished when he'd announced that his family would be staying in the north. Nowadays, his family embraced Ásta and even called upon her to translate when he was too busy.

"Dada," Johá squealed, his wide smile showing off the dimple in his chubby cheeks.

Dànel strode toward his little family, his heart filled with a satisfaction that none of his raiding adventures could ever match. Nothing compared to what he felt holding his son in his arms...except having his wife's long slender legs wrapped around his back. His manhood jumped at the image that flashed in his mind. Nightfall could not come soon enough for his liking.

"Let me help." He took the rope from Ásta and pulled the sled up the hill to their home.

"Dada." Johá reached for him with outstretched arms. The boy was entirely too used to being carried around.

"You spoil him, Ásta."

Tucking her fiery tresses behind her ear, she smiled softly. "He has his father's eyes—I cannot deny him."

Placing his son on the ground, he pointed at the puppy sniffing around the stump of an old pine tree. "It's time to give your mother a rest now. Go play with Jaská."

Johá squealed and ran toward the fluffy new addition to the family.

Dànel smiled affectionately, then turned and strode toward his wife. "Now that spring is coming, I want to take you and Johá out on the ice."

"Are you sure?"

"Já. Two winter ago, the thought would have terrified me, but I have made peace with losing Tóra." It had been a long painful journey to forgive himself. He had been shocked when his Aunt Tuá revealed that his fostering had been organized many months before Torá died. And his Aunt had been horrified that he thought he had been sent away because he thought they blamed him. Nobody, she had assured him, not even his father, blamed him for her death.

"It is time. I want teach our son the ways of his people, and you too." He knew that Ásta would love lying on the ice and listening to the singing sounds it made as it thawed. Sometimes he wondered if she loved this wild land more than he did.

"When you look at me like that you know I would give you anything," she said, pushing him playfully.

"You cannot deny me?" he teased, pulling her into his arms.

"I stopped trying long ago." She wrapped her arms around his waist and laid her head on his chest.

A smattering of snow began to fall as they stood watching Johá play with the boisterous puppy.

"He's growing so fast," Ásta said.

"Já. Are you weary?" He wondered if she had realized yet that she was with child? His smile broadened at the thought of her heavy with his child once more.

"Not as weary as you shall soon be, husband." Ásta looked up at him, her eyes burning with carnal promise.

His blood heated and his breeches became considerably more uncomfortable.

"Later," he promised, and then brushed his lips over hers.

Later he would make love to his warrior queen.

AFTERWORD

Thank you so much for reading Ásta and Dànel's story. I hope you had a wonderful time with them. Authors love reviews. If you enjoyed this book, please consider leaving a review at your place of purchase. If you enjoyed Winter Viking, you'll love the other Viking Hearts novellas. Read on for a sneak peek!

Beloved Viking

The shield-maiden must marry...

Heir to her father's Jarldom, Rúna Isaksson will soon ascend to replace him as leader, but first she must marry a warrior from another clan to form a powerful alliance. When her father creates a contest to determine the strongest suitor, Rúna demands to compete as well—if she wins, she can choose her own husband. However, she's shocked to discover that her first love is amongst the competitors, the man who abandoned her without looking back. She must not let him win.

A Viking warrior haunted by a dark past...

Jorvan Eriksson has returned from seeking his fortune to claim his childhood sweetheart, but the girl he left behind has become a battle-hardened shield-maiden with no intention of forgiving him. Jorvan has changed too—he now fights a darkness that lurks in his own mind. Somehow, he must conquer his demons to out-manoeuvre the other suitors and win the Viking games for Rúna's hand. Though victory alone will never be enough. He won't settle for anything less than reclaiming the future Jarl's heart.

Forbidden Viking

An Arabian Princess tastes freedom...

When Samara Abbasid's ship is attacked, she throws herself overboard and seeks refuge in the Viking Jarldom of Gottland. Claiming to be merely a scribe, she temporarily escapes her life of duty and expectation, and is free to sample the Vikings ways. She finds them as seductive as the strong Jarl, Valen. However, if Valen discovers her royal status he could use her as leverage in his trade negotiations with her father, the powerful Caliph. Worse, she must soon return to the royal court and her upcoming arranged marriage. But once she's tasted forbidden pleasure will she be able to return to a life of duty...?

A Jarl bound by duty...

The most powerful Viking clans are assembling on the isle of Gottland to celebrate Valen Eriksson's ascension to Jarl. So Valen is furious to discover rogue Vikings have raided in his territory. Now he must serve swift justice and protect the mysterious survivor until he can return her the Abbasid Caliph. The last thing he needs is to be tempted by the alluring scribe, not when he's sworn to choose a bride from an allied Viking clan. His duty is clear, yet his heart yearns...